THE FORGETTING CURVE

THE FORGETTING CURVE

BY ANGIE SMIBERT

Marshall Cavendish

No part of this publication may be reproduced, stored in a retrieval system, or transmitted, in any form or by any means, electronic, mechanical, photocopying, recording, or otherwise, without the prior permission of the copyright owner. Request for permission should be addressed to the Publisher, Marshall Cavendish Corporation, 99 White Plains Road, Tarrytown, NY 10591. Tel: (914) 332-8888, fax: (914) 332-1888. Website: www.marshallcavendish.us/kids

This book is a work of fiction. Names, characters, places, and incidents are products of the author's imagination and are used fictitiously. Any resemblance to actual events or locales or persons, living or dead, is entirely coincidental.

Other Marshall Cavendish Offices: Marshall Cavendish International (Asia) Private Limited, 1 New Industrial Road, Singapore 536196 • Marshall Cavendish International (Thailand) Co Ltd. 253 Asoke, 12th Flr, Sukhumvit 21 Road, Klongtoey Nua, Wattana, Bangkok 10110, Thailand • Marshall Cavendish (Malaysia) Sdn Bhd, Times Subang, Lot 46, Subang Hi-Tech Industrial Park, Batu Tiga, 40000 Shah Alam, Selangor Darul Ehsan, Malaysia

Marshall Cavendish is a trademark of Times Publishing Limited

Library of Congress Cataloging-in-Publication Data
Smibert, Angie.
 The forgetting curve / by Angie Smibert. — 1st ed.
     p. cm. — (Memento Nora)
 Summary: Tells, in separate voices, of a near future in which Winter
Nomura has had a psychotic break, and her friend Velvet and cousin Aiden,
who is visiting from his Swiss boarding school, try to uncover and fix what
is seriously wrong with their society, city, and even Aiden's family.
 ISBN 978-0-7614-6265-1 (hardcover) — ISBN 978-0-7614-6266-8 (ebook)
[1. Memory—Fiction. 2. Government, Resistance to—Fiction. 3.
Terrorism—Fiction. 4. Science fiction.] I. Title.
 PZ7.S63986For 2012
 [Fic]—dc23
 2011033038

Book design by Alex Ferrari
Editor: Marilyn Brigham

Printed in China (E)
First edition
10 9 8 7 6 5 4 3 2 1
mc Marshall Cavendish

To Dad, who always believed

I BLAME THE UNIVERSE

AIDEN NOMURA

It all started with a door.

Just like this one, but in a different city, in what feels like a different lifetime—even though it was only a month ago.

That day, I was standing there gawking like a damn tourist in front of this sleek, new glass storefront on Kramgasse when I heard the universe whisper to me.

Yeah, I said the universe. Call it Fate or The Force or whatever you want. Everything is everything. It's all part of one big system. I like to think of it as the universe.

And sometimes it whispers to me, like an old man backseat driving in the dark recesses of my brain. Sometimes the old fart mutters. Sometimes I can't tell what it's saying no matter how hard I listen. Today the universe was crystal clear.

Open that door. It changes everything.

I didn't know about it being a game-changer, but that door with those three letters etched on it definitely had a higher hack value than most shit in Bern.

This city is all cathedrals, medieval clock towers, cobble-stone alleys, and Alps. (Oh, and banks, but Mom made me promise not to touch the family business—not hers, at least.)

Of course, that's why Mom and Dad sent me to Bern American Academy: low temptation value. That, and no Coalition bombings. Ever. Switzerland has remained carefully neutral in everything.

I still found plenty of doors to rattle here. That's what I do. I pull on doors—on structures, in code, in social situations—until something opens. The universe usually nudges me in the right direction. Sometimes. Other times I just get into a shitload of trouble.

This door sent a shiver down my spine, even though I was sipping a huge latte with a double shot of espresso from the bakery across the street. I needed my caffeine and sugar fix before Trig class.

The etched glass door read TFC.

These guys understand hack value. They've phished their way into our collective gray matter. At least in the States.

But this was the first Therapeutic Forgetting Clinic in all of Switzerland. Right here two blocks from my school.

And not a soul was going in. Some locals even crossed

to the other side of the street rather than walk past the door. My cousin Winter said these places are all over Hamilton now, the whole US in fact. Europe—aside from the UK and Germany—not so much.

I couldn't imagine shit so bad you'd need to wipe it from your cerebral cortex.

I reached for the door handle.

Inside, the clinic was very un-clinic like: all bright colors and glossy café tables, which made the place look more like a McD's or Starbucks. Toward the back was a high counter with a large screen behind it. The screen was now hawking the Nomura Chipster.

Living over here, I forget sometimes about the damn ad algorithms. In the States, all the advertising, whether you're watching a 'cast or riding the bus, was keyed to your identity and shopping profile (same thing really). And that info was on your mobile or an ID chip. Still, it wasn't like I'd *buy* my own family products. I had the beta model of the Chipster in my pocket.

A cute blonde head popped up from behind the counter. *"Guten Morgen,"* she said with an uneasy smile before launching into her spiel in crappy German. I let her go on for a bit. She glanced down at something in her hand every few sentences, and her accent was obviously American.

Finally, her little speech ground to a halt, and she looked at me expectantly with her doelike brown eyes. They were open windows begging me to crawl in.

"What part of Georgia are you from?" I asked in English. No sense prolonging her agony.

"Oh, thank goodness." Relief slid over her face. "I'm from Macon, but I'm going to school in Atlanta. This is just a summer internship." She flipped her hair and smiled.

"Really?" I leaned into the counter toward her. This indicates interest. Social engineering 101. Flirt. It gets your foot in the door.

"Oh, yes. TFC flies us over so we can help set up all these new branches that are opening this summer. I'm a marketing major. We're supposed to learn customer service and stuff." She glanced around the shop as if unsure what other stuff she might learn here in Bern.

"So have you had many customers yet?" I knew the answer was no, but small talk could lead to other, hidden doors revealing themselves.

"We've been open since Saturday, and would you believe you're my first customer?" She looked me over again. "You are eighteen, aren't you? Otherwise you need a parent or guardian." She leaned toward me, clearly thinking (hoping?) I was her age.

"Oh yes, I'm nineteen. I'm in university here." Lie. Misrepresent. Make them trust you.

Above the girl, the screen was running a TFC ad. Clouds parted, unveiling blue skies, green pastures, and fluffy white sheep. *Forget your cares.* Could the symbolism be any more obvious?

I nodded toward the screen. "So how does this work?"

She laughed and tossed her hair again. "You're obviously American. Where have you been living? Under a rock?"

"Here," I said. "Same thing." Commiserate.

"Too true." She shook her head.

She'd probably been hoping to be posted to London or Paris or at least Zurich, not quaint little Bern. It's the capital, but still.

"Okay. Here's the deal. You go back in that little room, tell the doc the memory that's keeping you up at night, pop a pill—and go on like nothing ever happened. And you earn forgetting points each time you come in." She twirled a strand of blonde hair around her finger. "Maybe I could help you spend those points. You could show me around . . ."

The whole consumer-as-sheep scene behind her dissolved into a map of Europe. Red dots blossomed across the western half.

"How many branches is TFC opening here in Europe?" I asked as I wrote down a phone number. It wasn't mine; she was a little too cheerleader-ish for me.

She shrugged. "There's some rollout this summer in the States—something really big—and I think they want most of Western Europe to have a TFC by fall."

The screen above her head actually answered my question. *Thirty branches opening this summer. More in the fall.* The rest of EU sprouted red spots across its face.

"I'm Sandy, by the way." Her hand lingered over mine as I slid her the slip of paper. I smiled.

My mobile buzzed. It was Mom. "I gotta take this," I told Sandy and stepped away from the counter. She pouted for a second and then answered her own mobile.

"I'm okay. Has anything happened there?" Mom sounded breathless.

"That's nice, Mom, and nothing ever happens here . . ." I trailed off.

The 'cast on the big screen behind the counter cut to a scene of cops and billowing smoke and a barricaded street. Sandy scrambled to turn up the volume.

"Aiden?" There was panic in Mom's voice.

"What happened?"

"There was a car bombing in Zurich about three blocks from our offices."

A car bombing? Here? In Switzerland? War hasn't touched this place since, oh, Napoleon. This wasn't going to be pretty.

"Stay at school. I need to call your father."

Click.

Several passersby, all reading from their mobiles, crowded into the TFC to watch the newscast on the big screen. Smoke poured from several cars parked outside the Banc Suisse building in downtown Zurich. Mom's bank was down Bahnhofstrasse, only a block from the scene.

My mobile buzzed again. This time it was an emergency message from the headmaster. *All students are required to return to campus immediately.*

I guess if I were still living in the States, a little car bombing wouldn't be a big deal. That's why they have so many TFCs; there's always stuff happening there that you might want to forget.

I headed back out to the street. The locals were walking briskly, eyes focused on their mobiles as they made their way home. A few tourists, probably American by the look of them, shook their heads as shop after shop closed. A few minutes ago the cobblestones had seemed so peaceful and boring.

I missed it already.

I made like a local, too. I clicked through newscasts on my mobile as I walked toward school. The bombing outside the bank headquarters wasn't the only one.

I stepped off the curb to cross the street, and a hand yanked me back just as a black van barreled through the intersection. The van sped off and disappeared into an alley. I don't know what shocked me more: the hand or the van. This section of the Old Town is off limits to private vehicles. Only buses and cabs are allowed.

The hand belonged to a burly Asian man in a black suit. It took a moment for his face to register.

"Jao?" He's one my father's favorite bodyguards/drivers, a former Muy Thai champ. "What are you doing in Bern?"

Dumb question. Dad sent him to watch over me. Ichiro Nomura was paranoid that way. Now that I thought about it, Jao or another of Dad's minions had probably been lurking in the shadows ever since I came to Bern three years ago.

"You need to return to school, Master Aiden." Jao indicated the direction I was already going.

"That's what I was doing. How long have you been here?"

"Your mother will be here soon." He pointed toward school again.

That's when I heard the explosion. Seconds later I felt a rumble under my feet, and smoke started to pour out from the street behind us.

Jao pushed me toward school, and we took off running, the universe muttering something about black vans as the debris nipped at our heels.

ALL I GOT WAS A STUPID BOOK

AIDEN

"It was only some freaking car bombs," my roomie, Chase Loudon, complained. He stepped around the imposing form of Jao, who was standing vigil outside our dorm room. Chase was from Manhattan.

"I know." I shrugged. I really didn't feel that non-chalant, but in prep school, you have to act as if shit never touches you—even if you're covered in it. Other-wise, kids like Chase might think you don't belong, whether or not your father owns the biggest mobile company in North America and your mom runs an inter-national bank. "I didn't know Dad had him shadowing me."

"My father probably had me microchipped at birth." Chase chuckled, but it was probably true. "No, I meant the school, the Swiss, the world. *Quelle* overreaction."

The Loudons own Security Home Depot. They live in an über-exclusive vertical compound on the Upper East Side. The tower has its own shops, security, and even schools. Yet the Loudons, who make their billions on home security, didn't think their precious heir apparent was safe enough there.

At least that's what Chase told everyone.

I happen to know that ole Chase Evers Loudon III got expelled from Trump Day School for sexually harassing a teacher. (Our headmaster's administrative assistant really shouldn't use her cat's name as a password.)

But it wasn't just a couple of car bombs. Chase and I spent a mind-numbing hour watching newscasts. BBC World Interactive showed at least one car bomb had gone off in about thirty cities across Europe. Luckily, no one died, and the damage was minimal.

I tried to call Winter a few times but couldn't get through.

The universe was silent, too.

Mom pushed her way into our room.

"*Mäuschen*, are you okay?" She hugged me.

Chase mouthed the word "MILF" and made an obscene thrusting gesture behind her back.

"Fuck off," I mouthed to him. Chase can be a sucky human being even at the best of times. And this was not one of them.

He cleared his throat. "I'll just see if we have any mail." As Chase let himself out, I could see another man standing by Jao in that same bodyguard, eyes-straight-ahead, don't-mess-with-me stance.

"Mom, please." I grappled to retain a little dignity in her clutches. But I was relieved that she was in one piece. "You got here fast."

"Aiden, I was on my way to talk with you about something else when the whole world went crazy." Mom smoothed out her impeccable black suit. She called it her work uniform. With her clients, she had to look powerful yet elegant, understated, and discreet.

The world was already crazy, I wanted to say. Instead I said, "You shouldn't be driving or flying today."

"I took the bank's private jet service and brought Gunter." He's her favorite driver/bodyguard. She let out a long sigh. "I'm not going to change how I live because of this."

"Yeah, right." I crooked my thumb in Gunter's direction.

Mom waved away my concern and dropped into the only clean chair in the room.

To be fair, Mom's family had lived with private jets and bodyguards for eons. Not because of the Coalition, but because the family owns the second-largest private bank in Switzerland, a place renowned for its private financial dealings. And my mom, Gretchen Krieger Rausch, runs the mergers and acquisitions division of Banc Rausch.

Chase is damned lucky. Mom might look all Teutonic blonde, but if she'd seen that little move Chase made behind her back, he would've walked out of here minus a body part. Even her brothers are scared of her.

Something had brought my mother to Bern, something she didn't want to tell me over the phone. Maybe she and Dad were getting divorced after all. When they first sent me here, I thought that meant they were splitting up. Three years have gone by, and nothing. Yet.

"What is it?" I pushed some clothes off my bed.

"It's your cousin Winter. She's not hurt or anything like that," she added quickly. "But she is in the hospital."

I sank down on the mattress.

"Winter hasn't handled her parents being away as well as we thought. And her grandfather lets her run wild. Your father said it's possible she wasn't taking her medication. Now she's had a psychotic break."

"A what?" Psychotic? My Winter? I didn't believe it.

Mom explained that the doctor, a new one Dad found for her, thinks Winter may be schizophrenic. Paranoid schizophrenic, in fact. She'd thrown herself into her "weird" art, wasn't doing well in school, and was saying some crazy things about Uncle Brian and Aunt Spring's whereabouts.

"Like what?" I asked, though I wasn't sure I wanted to know.

"*Mäuschen*," Mom said in her best Mom-to-five-year-old voice. "Schizophrenia is a chronic mental illness where you lose touch with reality. Paranoid schizophrenics have delusions that everyone is after them or that the government is watching them. In Winter's case, she said the government took her parents and locked them up in a secret prison."

"*Scheisse*," I half-whispered.

Winter and I never really talked about her parents. Her friends—Micah and Velvet, yes. And her grandfather, whom she adores. We even talked about Jet, the woman she has a crush on. Not her parents. She did say once (twice?) that she didn't want to talk about them—too many people listening. I figured she'd said that because Uncle Brian and Aunt Spring were in Japan working on a super-secret project for the company. That's what Dad said when he took me skiing that Christmas. He also told me to keep it hush-hush so a competitor wouldn't pick up the info. And Mom had said not to bring it up because Winter was upset she got left behind. So I never pushed it.

Maybe I should have.

"Did you notice anything?" Mom asked. Sometimes her mom-radar was a little too accurate.

I shook my head. "She seemed fine all the times we've chatted."

Actually, we hadn't talked much in the last few weeks. But we did that sometimes. One of us would get sidetracked by a new project—hers are far more constructive than mine—and a month or two might go by before we checked in again. I should've known something was wrong this time, though.

"I know you two are close. That's why I wanted to tell you in person. In case you tried to call her." Mom hesitated, which is so unlike her. She leaned forward. "Aiden, you'd tell me if something was wrong, wouldn't you?" She peered at me the way she probably did over the negotiation table, trying to read my tells.

Suddenly I knew what this trip was all about. She could have called me about Winter. Mom wanted to reassure herself that me being away from her and Dad for so long hadn't cracked me, too.

"I know you and your father don't always get along, but—"

"The universe abides, Mom." I cut her off because I didn't want to hear her spiel about my hacking being all about getting Dad's attention.

She peered at me over her skinny black glasses. Okay, maybe my usual response wasn't the best one considering she was doubting my sanity.

"I'm fine, Mom." I smiled. She was still doing the peering thing at me, so I added, "I'm just bummed about Winter."

"I know, *mäuschen*. Me, too." She looked down at her hands. "Koji should have seen it coming. Spring is furious at him."

Koji, Mr. Yamada, is Aunt Spring's father—and Winter's grandfather. She'd been living with him for the past three years.

Mom rose to her feet and dusted herself off. "You really

do need to clean in here, Aiden." She glanced around the room in disgust.

"Can I see her?" I hadn't physically seen Winter in years. I hadn't been back to Hamilton since I got shipped to Bern Academy. Dad came here for the holidays, and I usually spent summers in Zurich with Mom—or here in summer school.

"She'll probably be in the hospital for a few weeks, Aiden. We'll talk after the term is over, but your father still wants you to stay here this summer. Now, I need to fly back to Zurich and do some damage control."

With that, Mom pecked me on the cheek and made her exit, Gunter in tow.

• • •

Psychotic.

I couldn't wrap my head around that word. Winter was brilliant. Creative. Eccentric. Manic, even. But *psychotic*? She'd made incredible things out of Legos and old cell phones and duct tape when she was eight. At twelve, she'd built the winning design in the national robotics competition, the one where the 'bots had to navigate obstacles or battle each other—the challenge was different every year. I'd helped. Using a script I'd found on a Russian board (I was still a noob then), I hacked the program to shave corners off the course. It was a kludge; it worked but for all the wrong reasons. Winter, however, created the robot completely on her own in that crazy-intense way she had. Not *crazy* crazy. She just had a way of losing herself in what she was creating. I envied that.

Jao opened the door and let Chase in, a couple of opened packages tucked under his arm and a soda from the canteen in the other hand.

"I see we're down to one doorman again." Chase dropped a package on his desk. I could hear the clink of jars and the rustle of wrappers. "I cannot believe the school has the audacity to search our packages. The headmaster probably gets a cut. My smoked salmon better be in here." He flung a loosely rewrapped package on my bed. "All you got was a stupid book."

The torn paper flopped open to reveal a large book, *Kinetic Sculptures of the Twentieth Century.*

Only one person would be even remotely interested in this shit.

Winter.

The universe has impeccable timing.

Sometimes.

THE SOUND OF HUMMINGBIRDS DROWNING

WINTER NOMURA

My eyelids were like lead, and the world wouldn't come into focus. The wings of hummingbirds beat in the gaping chasm between my ears—where my brain should be. In the distance, I could hear the trickle of words seeping into my consciousness.

"You've been sick, Ms. Nomura," a kindly voice told me. "Go back to sleep and it'll all be better in the morning."

My eyes fluttered closed. I couldn't help sleeping.

I didn't dream. I just listened to the growing chatter of voices droning on inside my skull, filling the emptiness with a torrent of words.

Hospital.

Japan.

Mental breakdown.

Somewhere deep down, though, I knew where I really was.

The hummingbirds told me before they drowned in all the words. Then the words gelled into pudding.

10:03 PM. TWO WEEKS LATER. SOMEWHERE IN THE CITY OF HAMILTON . . .

Welcome to the MemeCast, citizens. I don't care what you call me. The MemeCaster. Van girl. Night crawler. Meme Girl. Whatever. You're gonna forget it someday, anyway.

That's how we're built.

We forget. We find out something big, act all shocked and outraged for a day or two as the implications soak into our smooth, little brains. Then something else— something shinier and prettier or bigger and badder—gets dangled in front of us. We move onto glossier things— and, without someone reminding us, we forget.

That's why I'm here. To remind you. Of what you may have already forgotten and what you may forget in the future.

First, the past.

Last month, three young people stumbled across something dark and dangerous in our city, something that most of us suspected deep down but were unwilling to give voice to. They showed us that a certain three-letter corporation and its minions are behind some of the car bombings in our fair metropolis.

"Hold, on, Meme Girl," you may be saying right now. "That's crazy talk. Why would TFC and these other companies blow up cars? Here, at home?"

The why is not too hard to fathom: they make money off our fear. When the real terrorism wasn't enough anymore to drive us to "buy buy buy," they created their own terror—but just enough to make us want to cocoon ourselves in a brand-new security blanket of stuff—and forget.

These kids caught a glimpse of the proverbial smoking gun—black van guys setting a bomb—and put it on paper—in the form of an underground comic. As a reward, they were carted off to Detention. The Big D, variety. You know it exists. And those kids were forced to tell their stories, day after day, until the drug—the same one that so many of you pop at the TFCs on every corner—bleached their brains of those events. Now they don't remember what they did for us. Neither do their friends and families.

And I bet most of you don't remember, either.

"But Meme Girl," you say. "I couldn't forget something like that."

Well, sometimes the forgetting curve isn't enough. Sometimes it needs a little help.

Now for your listening pleasure tonight, we'll start with the eleven-thousandth cover of an old ditty about the 'burbs: "Little Boxes," coming to you from the Sneetches. You know, even the children "are put in boxes / and they come out all the same."

4.0

THE CHIP
FAIRY COMETH

VELVET KOWALCYK

Do not wear fishnet stockings and a boiled wool skirt to a dank garage. Or any garage. In June. *Book of Velvet*. Chapter 47, Verse 233.

Obviously I don't read my own book because there I was, perched on a rusty John Deere riding mower in Spike's sweltering garage. The pits of my vintage Ramones T-shirt were sopping. And who is so damn lazy that they need a tractor to mow that postage stamp of green out there?

Anyway. Richie and Little Steven finally let Spike join the Wannabes. Their lead singer got drafted, and I suspect the boys secretly coveted this shack as a practice space.

And poor Spikey needed the practice. His voice sounded like a wounded animal's with gravel stuck in its throat.

The song wasn't helping. It had the emotional depth of Cheez Whiz. I could write a better song than that—if this weren't such a waste of time. The urban/folk/metal rage-against-the-machine thing the guys were striving for wasn't going to happen.

I so missed Winter—and Micah. My bangs were still blue, which Winter and I had done together before she went to the hospital. The darn Nomuras wouldn't let me see her. And then Micah ended up in juvie for god knows what. And now I'm stuck listening to this crap.

Summer is going to suck.

"Velvet! Earth to Velvet." The music had stopped, and Spike was bellowing at me instead of singing. Frankly, it was hard to tell the difference.

"What?" I growled.

"What did you think?" he asked so innocently.

Richie groaned.

"Dude, do not ask her. She'll tell you the truth," Little Steven said, throwing up his hands as if to deflect the shrapnel he knew was going to fly.

He was right. You ask, you'd better really want to know. You call, you'd better really want to talk. And if you ask me to hang out, you'd better have more in mind than sitting in your filthy garage.

"The words *water buffalo* come to mind," I said flatly.

Richie and Steven stifled a laugh. Spike looked crestfallen, but he sidled over to me.

"I thought we were going to do something," I told him as I dusted off my skirt.

"We are." He leaned in to kiss me, but I dodged the full-on bullet.

"No, *you're* doing something." I flicked a pigtail over my shoulder. *I'm just watching. As usual.* "Sitting on my ass in a sweatbox doesn't constitute doing something." I pecked him on the cheek and made for the exit.

"It's a nice ass," Spike called as I ducked under the rising garage door. "Well, it is," I heard him say to the boys.

Great. In school, I was the one with the weird clothes and blue hair. Now I'm the one with the nice ass.

Time to find something to do. Thing is, I had no clue what that was. So I just walked.

The slap of my boots on the pavement was a hypnotic sound that drowned out my dreary poor-me thoughts. Soon I found myself outside Black Dog Architectural Reclamation and Bakery—or at least what was left of it. Micah didn't like to let on that he lived there in the homeless village behind those concrete walls. But Winter said Black Dog Village was a really cool place.

Now, it was a burned-out hull decorated with yellow police tape. I can't believe I'm saying this, but I was glad that Micah was in juvie—and that his mom had gotten that TFC apartment—before all this happened. Still, it's hard to believe what the news said—that they found bomb-making materials here. Micah wouldn't knowingly live with Coalition terrorists; but I guess you never know your neighbors, even in a place like this.

"ID scan." Two cops had come up behind me while

I stared at the rubble. One tapped behind his ear.

Damn. They were checking for the new ID chips.

"We've still got a few weeks left in the grace period," I stammered as I fumbled in my pocket for my mobile. They'd have to accept the old ID until then, right? Trouble was, my parents were dead set against the new ID chips that had to be implanted in your skull. The compounds had been using implants for years, but now the city was making its own special chip mandatory.

I offered one of the cops my mobile. The officer with the scanner ignored me and swiped the device by my right ear. I tensed to hear the warning go off. Instead, the scanner chimed pleasantly.

"She's good," he told the other cop as if I wasn't even there. "Anne Marie Kowalcyk. Fifteen. 122 Walnut Avenue."

"Thank you for complying, Miss." The other cop handed back my mobile. "This new chip makes our lives so much easier." He nodded toward the remains of Black Dog.

I stood there like a stunned mullet while the cops rode off into the sunset. I'm good? Thank you for complying?

I felt behind my ear. *What the hell?* There was a raised disc under the skin. The damn chip fairy had visited me in my sleep. Not cool.

Thou shalt not stick shit in my skull (or any other part of my body) without express written permission. Maybe not even then. *Book of Velvet*. Chapter 1, Verse 1.

Someone had some explaining to do.

5.0

THE UNIVERSE COMES HOME TO ROOST

AIDEN

The glossy bit of code was as smooth as glass, with no place to grab onto, no hidden doors for me to rattle open. It was a hard nugget of gorgeousity. Mom thought it would keep me busy on the flight. Her bank thought it was the next wave in encryption: security in a tiny package.

Security isn't about code, though. It's about trust.

With a few clicks, I logged into the bank's database of employees and located a likely mark. Two calls, one message, and a little digital dumpster diving later, I'd convinced one of the software team members to divulge his password to the project source code. Most people trust a call from their own tech support.

And with the password, I found the key to unlock the code.

The actual key.

Information—whether it's money, messages, code, etc.—can be encrypted with a long string of characters called a key. And most encryption needs two keys. One locks, or encrypts, the information so it can be sent securely; another unlocks, or decrypts, the stream at the other end. The longer and more random each key is, the more secure it is. Sure, you can write a program to crunch through every possible combination of characters, but that kind of brute force attack can take weeks—even months.

Humans are always the weak link in the system. There's no security patch for us. We're hardwired to trust. Social Engineering 101.

I'd found only the decryption key in the bank's files, but that's all I needed.

Still, it was way too easy. And it didn't take my mind off what was in that book Winter had sent me, the book that was now stuffed into my backpack in the overhead bin. I didn't dare take it out on the plane. You never knew who was flying the unfriendly skies.

The flight attendant tapped me on the shoulder and made an unhappy face at my mobile. I flicked it off and shoved it into my backpack. We'd obviously come to the tray-tables-and-seats-in-their-upright-and-locked-positions part of the flight. We were on approach to Dulles.

• • •

Take-offs and landings make me a little jittery. Not for the obvious, we're-all-going-to-die reasons. No, if we crash, we crash. Everything is everything. But with my portable electronic devices stowed properly in my luggage, I only had the stupid ads to look at as they played across the seat-screen in front of me.

Of course, it was another ad for the mobile I'd just stuffed in my pack. A young guy rocked out to his Chipster in the shower sans earbuds. *The Nomura Chipster. It speaks to you.* Tacked onto the end of the ad was an announcement for a new app. *It'll be like having TFC right in your pocket. Take it back to school. Only on Nomura.*

The family biz. I wasn't looking forward to it.

The only way Dad would let me come home was if I interned at the company this summer. I'd played the prodigal son bit. I'd convinced him that my hacker ways were behind me, and all I wanted to do was learn the family biz and become the buttoned-down corporate prince he'd always wanted. I was amazed Dad bought it; he's usually way sharper than that.

I hadn't left him many options, I guess. Not after I got myself kicked out of Bern American last week. (And Switzerland wasn't proving to be the neutral safe haven it had always been.)

The pilot announced our final descent. Landings were worse than take-offs. At least during take-offs I could study the flight attendant dynamics—who was senior, who got along with whom, who flirted with the passengers, who had a mother complex, who was schmoozable, who I could charm into a free headset or a drink. It's all code.

People. Systems. Software. During landings, though, the attendants are all business. They're ready to get the hell off the plane. They've got husbands or hot dates or even just hot baths on their minds.

So that left me with too many idle processing cycles to crunch over the one piece of code I couldn't crack: me. Can source code do more than it's programmed to do? Can it peer down through its own layers to the assembly language and machine code underneath it? Can it change its very being? Whoa. Way too deep for business class.

I didn't want to think about Winter yet, either.

I pulled up the in-flight programming on the console in front of me. Most of it was fluff, so I flicked on the news. There was a Coalition bombing in Atlanta. A Hamilton security firm that was indicted for "unlawful counterterrorist activities" was cleared of all charges. (The firm was, in turn, suing the newscast that accused it of misconduct.) TFC announced a new housing program for the homeless. And TFC was also continuing to give away new ID chips to help less fortunate Hamiltonians comply with the new security requirements.

The forgetting people are just overflowing with altruosity all of a sudden, aren't they?

But the big story was some sex scandal with a congressman and a 'cast star I'd never heard of. Not that I'd heard of many. *There goes his reelection and his shot at being president*, the news reader said.

The pilot announced our final approach into Dulles.

I flicked off the screen and peered out the window. The plane banked just south of Washington. I could see the white glints of the monuments, the green ribbon of the Potomac, and the flat, ugly Pentagon squatting below it like a mushroom. Beyond all that, the plane flew over houses lined up on grids and circled with fences, fanning out as far as the eye could see.

Nomura had originally wanted to build its North American headquarters in the DC 'burbs. But my great-grandfather found a more tax- (and incentive-) friendly atmosphere in Hamilton, a satellite city not too far outside the beltway, a city that would be indebted to the Nomuras in a way that the sprawling metropolis of Washington, DC, never could be.

A half-dozen banks, TFC, and several other corporate players had the same idea. Now they all act like they own the city. They do, really. I mean, if you act like you're in charge and people go along with it, then you're in charge. It's all about the buy-in, the trust.

And we're a trusting people here in the US.

Con artists like that in a mark.

IN THE GARDEN OF THE GUINEA PIGS

WINTER

We were in a cab. The news flickered across the screen between us and the driver. The Action 5 News guy said it was a record: no Coalition bombings in Hamilton since May. The mayor attributed it to the new ID program. *Don't forget*, news guy added, *there's only two weeks left to get your new chip. Mayor Mignon said there'll be zero tolerance for noncompliance.* Then there was some Nomura ad, of course.

I scratched a bump behind my ear.

Wait. May? I pulled out my mobile. It was a slim, red model that I didn't recognize. I checked the date.

June 15. Where the hell had I been?

The cabbie let us off at the corner of Eighth and Day. My brain felt like pudding. The last thing I remembered, I told Grandfather, was working on the sculpture garden in the backyard.

Sculpture garden? he'd asked as if he didn't have a clue what I was talking about.

We pressed our way through the secret door in the back fence, through the *Sasuke* course, and through the bamboo gates into my garden.

Grandfather didn't say a word as he took in the Pawing Man, the Flailing Arm Windmill, and the Shopping Bag Crab. Those sculptures, I remembered creating. That masked thing with the monkey wrench and the gears, though, was a complete mystery to me. It was like a stranger had invaded my garden and finished it for me.

I wanted to be that person.

How do I put that last sculpture into words? It was as if a mask had been torn away from a face, revealing the clockworks underneath. The disturbing thing was that those gears were connected to something outside of it, like the person's brain was part of a bigger machine. It captured a feeling I knew I must have felt at one time, but it was like a memory of a memory. Like I'd seen it in a big, coffee-table book somewhere. It made me feel frenetic and serene all at once. Maybe it made me feel uncomfortable, too.

I'd started this garden to keep busy while my parents were away. Where had they gone? Something in my head whispered, *Japan*. That didn't sound right. The voice didn't sound like mine, either. Where have I been that I've missed creating these sculptures? *Hospital*, the voice whispered again.

I shook off the whisper. I didn't remember being in the hospital. I remembered working on the Flailing Arm Windmill, waiting for Micah to come over. Or was I waiting for Grandfather to get home?

I closed my eyes and tried to remember the first time I set foot in this garden.

• • •

I could hear steps—no, running—shoes slapping in time, running in place, over this whirring sound in my head. Grandfather led me by the hand through the bamboo gate into this smooth oval of sand crisscrossed with gleaming bamboo walkways. The sand was bare, and the sun was bright overhead. He told me to be quiet, and he'd be back for me. I was scared, but I don't remember why. I just remember the feeling—like something had been ripped away from me, or I from it. It was as if I had a big, gaping hole in the middle of me, and I just wanted to curl up and wrap myself around it, like a cocoon in the warm sun. I fought the urge for a while, listening for Grandfather or someone else to come, too scared to move. Eventually, I gave in to the feeling and fell asleep, my back pressed against the spot where the smooth walkways intersected. I dreamed of crazy, wonderful moving things growing in this garden.

Later, Grandfather gently prodded me awake.

"They've taken your mother and father, but you'll be safe with me, Win-chan," he said. "We'll get them back."

Taken.

• • •

I searched my brain for a memory of that word *taken*, of what had happened before I'd stepped into this garden, but it was like probing for a missing tooth with my tongue. It darted in and out of the empty space, finding only a hole where something solid should be.

The *step-whir* sound came flooding back to me then, drowning out the whispers that said *Japan* and *assignment*. The sound sped up like the wings of a hummingbird inside my head. It was an oddly comforting sound.

The hummingbird said it was all a lie. *The voices lie.*

My sculptures agreed.

I searched the gazebo and found the remote on the table behind the mask thing. I pressed the power button, and the Pawing Man slapped angrily at the water until it lapped up against the Shopping Bag Crab. The Crab crawled forward haltingly, weighed down by the bag it had made its home, only to falter at the top of the sand mound and slide back to where it started, defeated. The limbs of the Flailing Arm sculpture turned around their windmill, reaching for something at the apex, only to be dragged back down and around for another fruitless try. The cloth from the—uh, I wasn't quite sure what I'd called this one, but it looked like sails—the Sail Thing quivered in the breeze but didn't do much else. I remembered thinking about them, about making them into some sort of solar chime.

I pressed another button on the remote. An eerie cacophony of low-fidelity sounds came from the canvas of the Sail Thing. Ringtones and other annoying electronic sounds mixed together to make my skin tingle. It wasn't a soothing sound, but it captured a feeling I couldn't quite put my finger on.

Hummingbirds fluttered through my brain.

I needed to tinker with something.

My workshop off the garden was an old garage from back in the day before Grandfather's car blew up. He'd never replaced the car. Bits and pieces of plastic, wood, and metal cluttered my workbench inside. Rusted pipes and a few sticks of lumber lay on the floor, pushed off to the side of the room. Richie's backup guitar and amp rested on a side table. I guess I hadn't gotten around to modifying them before I went to the hospital. (The hummingbirds fluttered at that word.) I know I had a bunch of old cell phones, but they seemed to have evaporated from the shelves. The ancient computer that anchored my garden network still hummed under my workbench. The Scooby Doo lunch box I'd gotten at a swap meet was still there as well.

That's what I'd been thinking of doing with the sailcloth material from Grandfather's *Sasuke* course. I was going to sew the receivers into the cloth along with some solar-power cells—none of which were on the shelves, either—and make a kind of solar-powered chime. Okay, obviously I did that part already. But I'd also planned to build a low-power transmitter to control what played on the chimes.

That's why I bought the lunch box—to house the transmitter. I picked the box off the shelf. Technically, it was an antique, though Grandfather wouldn't like to hear that. (He'd liked the show as a kid, and it was ancient even way back then.) Something about the box had spoken to me. The turquoise and yellow tin was shaped like an old van, with the Scooby gang stuffed into the front seat and *The Mystery Machine* painted in reddish orange on the side. I don't know why this silly box made me smile, but it did. I pried off the lid with a little work, and I smiled even bigger.

I had built the transmitter.

Inside, an old music pod was hooked up to the transmitter. I flicked on everything and selected a song to play. "It All Falls Away" by U-238. The music shimmered out of the sails in the garden in a satisfyingly eerie way.

To my surprise, something vibrated in my pocket. I pulled out the red mobile and slid it open. The music from my sculpture exploded in my skull; it was as if I had a tiny speaker behind my right ear. I fumbled for the mobile and slid it closed. The music stopped ringing in my brain. I turned the mobile over in my hands. The words *Nomura Chipster* were scrawled across its outer shell. There was also some Kanji on the back, which probably meant it was a new model still being tested. We used to get these beta and pre-beta models all the time when Mom and Dad were home. A Nomura family perk. We were the guinea pigs for every new product.

I felt behind my ear where the sound seemed to have come from. Damn. While I was out, someone implanted a chip obviously designed to work with this stupid mobile.

Did Grandfather okay this? That was so not him.

I flipped off the transmitter and closed the Mystery Machine up tight. Why would my mobile pick up the sculpture's low-power transmission?

The hummingbirds grew louder in my head.

7.0

I PUT MY GAME FACE ON

AIDEN

As soon as we pulled up to the gate, I fished my mobile out of my pack. I had a message from Dad's secretary.

The limo will pick you up outside baggage claim. Your father will meet you at your cousin's house. She's coming home today.

No kidding.

I grabbed my bags and headed toward Customs. After an interminable wait on line, and sweating through what felt like a full-cavity search of bags and person, I found the limo waiting outside.

The driver asked if I wanted to stop for coffee or something to eat before we got on the interstate. I shook my head. An ad flickered across the privacy screen between us. The mayor of Hamilton, Albert Mignon, was running for Congress.

Utterly straight-faced, he told a young mother and child, "I'll never forget who I work for."

This ad paid for by the Patriot Party, a wholly owned subsidiary of TFC, the fine print said underneath the scene.

Yeah, I bet he never forgets, I thought.

I pulled Winter's book out of my backpack and flipped it open to the center. Security hadn't even looked twice at the old library book on kinetic sculptures of the last century. But inside, concealed in a hollowed-out section, was some truly modern art: a comic called *Memento*.

Something had told me not to take the comics out on the plane—or to let my roomy, Chase, see them. As soon as I discovered the stash, I'd grabbed the book and headed to the bathroom down the hall.

The ink on the simple black-and-white pages still smelled fresh.

In one comic strip, a girl goes to TFC. In the waiting room, she sees a boy spitting out his pill. Then she hears her mom's awful secret and decides to spit out her own pill in order to remember. In the second comic, a kid on a skateboard gets hit by a black van. In another, the same skateboarder sees people from a black van set what looks like a bomb on a car; the car has another kid in it. The van leaves and goes to a place marked Soft Target. The skateboarder saves the other kid before the car blows up.

It all made a good story.

Soft Target, I found out, was a real company, a Hamilton

security corp that had gone bankrupt recently but had reformed under a new name: Green Zone. But that didn't mean anything. It was just a story.

I almost filed the comics away in the maybe-Winter-is-crazy file when I ran across something else. It didn't take me too long to find, but only because I used an open-source search before I left Bern. You can't do those searches in the States anymore; you can search only corporate-scrubbed data. I found a newscast of a girl, Nora James, who claimed to be one of *Memento*'s authors, being carted off by security. The reporter, Rebecca Starr, was later axed by the 'cast. (She had a very hot tiger tattoo reaching over her shoulder.) They probably both got brain-bleached.

This was heavy stuff, if it were true. But I still didn't get why Winter would send it to me—right before going into the hospital. She wouldn't be part of anything like this. She wasn't Miss Get-Involved. She'd have to like people for that.

Still, I left a few *Memento*s in the bathroom stalls at school before my timely departure. It seemed like the thing to do, and the universe agreed. I also posted the video to everyone's mobile at Bern American using the school's emergency distribution system—you know, the one they use to alert everyone about blizzards and avian flu outbreaks. Call it a parting gift.

* * *

Outside the window, the suburbs gave way to stretches of green, broken up by the occasional big-box store and gated compound. More damn ads streamed across the screen in front of me. Nomura. TFC. AmSwiss Air. Mayor Mignon. Green Zone. Starbucks. Insert random corporati. It all blurred together.

. . .

Finally, we rolled into Hamilton. The limo driver locked the doors as soon as we exited the interstate and headed into a seedier looking part of downtown. A bombed-out car sat rusting on the curb not two blocks from where we stopped. I could see why Mom wanted me to stay in Switzerland and try the school in Montreaux. She had the pull to get me in wherever. But I'd wanted to come home. Now I found myself homesick for Bern, with its cathedral, the medieval clock tower with the moving puppets, the museums, and the Garden of Roses, all in the shadows of the snowy peaked Alps. Suddenly Bern didn't seem so cheesy.

"Is this it?"

Winter's home was an old warehouse, at least on the outside. Uncle Brian and Aunt Spring both worked in Research and Development at Nomura. And they were Nomuras, after all. I guess I was expecting a high-rise building with an uzi-toting doorman and valet parking.

Then I remembered. Winter had been living with her grandfather. Koji Yamada owns several tattoo parlors in

Hamilton. I bet this was his idea of a bohemian, artsy kind of place, and it was probably near one of his shops.

"Your father said for you to wait in the car until he gets here." The driver glanced nervously up and down the street. He kept the motor running and the doors locked.

A few minutes later, another limo pulled up beside ours. The doors unlocked. "I'll take your bags home, Master Aiden," the driver said.

Jao, who was driving Dad's Bradley, opened the doors of both limos and watched the street as I slid from one vehicle to the other. Dad had rotated Jao home shortly after the day of the bombings; two of Mom's goons stuck to me like snow on an Alp right up to when she put me on the plane.

"You had an uneventful flight. I didn't hear of any computers crashing while you were over the Atlantic." Ichiro Nomura allowed himself an upturned corner of a smile. My father is not humorless; he just seldom lets that side of him slip out from under his composed salary-man mask—unless it serves his purpose. Now his purpose was to chastise his wayward son and to remind him who was boss on this side of the Atlantic.

"Jet lag," I said with the same half-smile on my face. "After a little sleep and some non-airplane food, I'll be rattling those doors again."

"The only doors you'll be rattling this summer are to the lab and your room." All trace of humor was gone from his face as he got out of the car. He strode toward the house without waiting for me.

Dad can't get away from me fast enough.

I grabbed my backpack and hurried after him.

Mr. Yamada looked a little surprised to see us when he opened the door. He acknowledged Dad with the slightest of head bows. I saw Dad stiffen slightly, but not enough for anyone else to catch it.

"We just got home ourselves," Mr. Yamada said, more to me than to Dad. Winter's grandfather waved us into the loft. It was the kind of place I imagined he and Winter would live: wide-open space, minimal furniture, industrial-looking pipes overhead, concrete floors, and artwork everywhere. Oh, and an old motorcycle in the foyer.

Dad took in the place, too, but I don't think he was appreciating its aesthetic value. "If you'll pardon me, Koji, I'll call Brian to see where they are," he said.

Mr. Yamada motioned him toward the leather sofas at the other end of the loft. To me he said, "She's in the garden." He nodded toward an enormous Shoji-screen door at the back of the house.

Winter had told me about her garden. I knew she'd built several moving sculptures within the traditional Japanese garden—bamboo, sand, rocks—that Mr. Yamada had started. But even after seeing pics of one or two of the sculptures, I had trouble visualizing it.

The Shoji screen door, I realized as I got closer, wasn't made of rice paper and bamboo. It was made out of Kevlar and had an R39 security system attached to it.

The door swooshed open, and I couldn't move for a

moment. The gleaming bamboo walkways and white sand were so serene, so cliché-Japanese; but the sculptures were so stark and industrial, all burnished metal, with splashes of plastic, cloth, and paint. The whole thing tore at me, like my own two sides.

"Wow," I whispered.

The sculptures sprung to life as I stood there gawking. Arms started turning. The sail-things tinkled. The metal guy slapped the water. He reminded me of a fountain I'd seen in Zurich or Basel. But I'd never seen anything like that shopping bag crab thing. It pulled itself along with windshield wiper legs. The whole thing worked together like a mad machine.

Staggering. Genius. Warped—in a good way.

Of course, buttoned-up engineering and financial types—like our parents—might see craziness in Winter's creativity. Our family knew how to make money, not art. Then again, a lot of famous artists had mental problems. Van Gogh was bipolar or schizophrenic—I forget which.

I stumbled around peering at each creature, trying to figure out how she'd done it. Then I got to the pagoda. The mask sculpture in the middle of the table stopped me. Scaffolding held the mask in place, but its façade had eroded in spots, revealing the gear works underneath. The thing unnerved me. It was like someone had tried so hard to keep up a front because they were afraid to let people see beneath the mask, but it fell away, anyway. It was so deep I felt like I was drowning.

A song began playing from the sail sculpture. And my mobile started vibrating. It was probably Mom calling to see if I got here okay. I fished the mobile out of my pocket, and I was going to answer it, but I caught a glimpse of Winter through an open door off of the pagoda. She was tinkering with a lunch box.

What if she *was* sick? What if she was different? I put on my own mask, hoping the holes weren't revealing too much, and stepped through the doorway.

8.0
UNTAKEN

WINTER

"Winter?" a voice said from the direction of the garden. The hummingbirds quieted so I could hear. It was a male voice, but not Grandfather's or anyone else I immediately recognized. "Winter?" the voice said again, this time closer.

I turned to see a young man standing in the entrance from the garden. It took a second for it to click. I hadn't seen Aiden in the flesh since my parents left. And he'd grown. About a foot and a half, at least.

My cousin crossed his arms over his very preppy sweater vest, which he was wearing on top of a snowy white T-shirt and jeans. The sweater had some sort of crest on it. A few years ago, he'd been sent away to a Swiss boarding school near where his mother lived.

"Nice outfit," I said. It wasn't.

"The shit in this garden is genius," he said, matching my farthest-thing-from-the-truth tone. He scoped out the workshop with this practiced mask of indifference plastered across his face. That face must have been very useful in boarding school.

He didn't fool me. Nothing bored him.

"Oh, shut up," I said. "You know it is."

His mask cracked, revealing the true Aiden, the one I'd always seen no matter what face he put on for the rest of the world. His hazel eyes looked green under the fluorescents.

"Damn, girl." He tucked a strand of black hair behind his ear and grinned. "It's really good to see you."

We hugged. I asked him about school.

"Oh, let's not talk about that dreariness." He was picking through things on my workbench like a hungry dog sniffing out treats. "Tell me about that." He pointed at my garden. "It really is genius." He handed me the remote. "Show me." This was my Aiden, wide-eyed, eager to figure it all out, to tear everything apart and put it back together his own way.

I couldn't think of anything I'd rather do than show him my creations. I pushed the button on the remote and the sculptures came to life.

"I got your message," Aiden said as he took my arm.

"What message?"

"You know, the book, the *Memento*s." He whispered this last part as we crossed the threshold into the garden.

I had no clue what he was talking about.

Then I saw her.

My mother—Spring Nomura—stood in the center of the garden, in the pagoda, in the flesh, smiling, teary-eyed, the whole surprise-I'm-home works. I ran into her arms like I was still that kid who'd hidden in the garden so many years ago. My good dreams were all about this.

"Winter, honey. It's okay," she said as she stroked my hair. "I'm here now. We're home for good."

"We?" I looked around. Aiden had melted back into the workshop, where I could see him gingerly shaking my Scooby Doo lunch box. There was no one else in the garden.

"Of course, silly. Your father's trying to find a safe place to park. This neighborhood," Mom said with a shudder in her voice. "I didn't realize it had gotten so rough. It's no wonder Father got hurt on his neighborhood patrol."

"Hurt?" Not my Sasuke-san. I felt a lump of panic rising in my throat. He'd seemed okay when we both stumbled out of the cab. I turned toward the kitchen.

"He's fine now, dear. Don't you remember?" Mom took my hand. "He was in the hospital, too. Just a concussion, but at his age, you can't be too careful." She shook her head sadly. "We should have taken you with us."

"Taken me with you?" I was puzzled but not sure why.

"To Japan, of course." She looked at me warily. "The schools are so much better there. Everything is so clean."

The hummingbird wings fluttered in my ears.

"Why didn't you take me?" I backed away.

"Oh, honey," she said sadly. "You know why. You didn't want to go. You didn't want to leave your friends or your grandfather. And," she added in a hushed voice, "your doctor didn't think it was a good idea."

Doctor? I didn't know what doctor she was talking about. Did she mean the shrink? I didn't start seeing her until after they left. Then again, I didn't even remember why I'd been in the hospital.

What was going on? I looked at Mom again, this time with my X-ray vision, as my friends liked to call it. Mom was older, thinner maybe, and as neatly dressed as ever. I knew I hadn't seen this woman in years.

"Baby, are you feeling okay?"

"Fine," I said. "Just tired, I guess." It wasn't the time to grill her.

"Not too tired to give your dad a hug," my father said as he walked through the door from the house. He was older, too; his short shock of black hair was sprinkled with more gray than I remembered. He had the same thin black glasses, though.

Inside my head, the hummingbirds fluttered, but the little voice whispered over them. *Yes, they were in Japan working for the company. But they're home now. Everything is finally okay. You can get on with your life. Forget about art and hummingbirds. Work hard. Go to school. A good school. Work for the company.* I don't know where that came from.

"Ah, Pooh-bear, I've missed you." Dad wrapped me in

a hug, and I was too tired to fight the voices. I was just happy to have my parents home again.

When I emerged from Dad's arms, I could see we'd been joined by Grandfather, Aiden, and his father. My uncle looked exactly the same every time I'd seen him, which wasn't often: all business. Black hair, black tie, black suit. He's the head of Nomura North America. Only *his* father, Katsu, the chairman of the Nomura Corporation in Japan, outranked Ichiro Nomura.

My other grandfather, Koji Yamada, laid out a tea tray on the small table in the pagoda. I flicked off the kinetic sculptures. Grandfather handed me a thick black coffee with—I knew without tasting it—six sugars. He'd made green tea for everyone else.

They sipped tea politely, not saying anything for a long moment. Aiden finally broke the ice.

"The garden is spectacular, isn't it?"

My mother and father exchanged glances. Mom glared at Grandfather as he stared into his teacup. Uncle Ichiro took a sip of his tea before commenting that I showed "quite a mechanical aptitude."

"She could always build anything with her hands." Aiden nodded in agreement as if his father had been the one to bring up the subject. "You know, Winter should intern with me at the company this summer. Robotics, maybe."

His father looked pleased at the idea. I couldn't tell if Aiden was working his dad or trying to divert attention from the obvious tension between my parents and Grand-father. Were they mad at him for something?

"That would be a more productive use of her time," Mom said, a harsh edge creeping into her voice. She kept glaring at Grandfather.

Aiden nudged me and his father toward the Shopping Bag Crab. "Father, you should see this one."

Ichiro raised an eyebrow but followed us. Aiden turned over the crab and examined its workings. My mother's voice fell into heated whispers directed at my Grand-father. Aiden blathered on about some program he'd hacked at school, but I couldn't help listening to the other conversation.

"Didn't you realize she wasn't taking her meds?" Mom asked.

Grandfather froze as if trying to remember some long ago information tucked in his brain. Eventually, he shook his head. I'd never seen him so unsure of himself, so meek. Normally, there was nothing meek or even remotely retired about my grandfather. He runs three tattoo shops, patrols the neighborhood for baddies, and works out on his *Sasuke* obstacle course.

"How could you not have known?" Mom gestured to the moving statues around her.

Grandfather didn't answer. And I didn't want to hear any more. They hated my garden. They thought it was some outward manifestation of inner crazy.

"Mom, stop it." I strode back to her. "He's not to

blame for anything." I touched Grandfather's hand, just above where the snake head emerged from his crisp white sleeve. The dress shirt couldn't camouflage all of his tats. A tiger's claw reached out of his other sleeve, and the cherry blossom—the tat that symbolized my mom's birth—peeked out from his collar. The only tattoo you couldn't see was the one that celebrated my birth: a snowflake over his heart. "He's always been here for me." I gave his hand a squeeze.

"Dad," my mother said sounding angrier than before. She tore my hand from his. "You promised." She held up the back of my hand for everyone to see.

"Spring, I did not do that." He turned to me.

A perfect circle had been tattooed on the fleshy part between my thumb and forefinger. It wasn't perfect really; it was more like someone had done it with a calligraphy brush in one stroke, not quite closing it. I stared at the circle. Nothing came to me.

"I don't remember," I said slowly. I wanted to say I didn't remember a lot of things—them leaving, them ever calling or visiting, me going to the hospital, or anything that happened in the last few weeks. The hummingbirds flitted wildly.

"It's okay, honey," she said acting motherly all of a sudden. She took my hand in hers and spoke slowly and calmly, like she was speaking to a five-year-old. "The doctor said you might have some holes in your memory. It's one of the side effects of treatment."

"Ichiro has arranged for you to see an excellent doctor at the compound," my father said, finally joining the conversation.

"Compound?" I asked dumbly.

"Tamarind Bay. Ichiro got us a new house there, near his. And you're already enrolled in school for the fall."

Great, I thought. A compound. And a new school. I had friends *here*. Finally. Before I moved in with Grandfather, we'd lived in an old-fashioned 'burb on the south side of town. Southern Hills wasn't a compound, but everyone there was on a waiting list to get into one. *Same difference*. I had zero in common with those kids.

"A summer internship wouldn't be a bad idea," Dad said.

His brother nodded. "We have an opening." It had probably been his idea. Maybe he was the one playing Aiden.

My life was all arranged, at least for the foreseeable future, by my loving family that was suddenly back in my life. It was almost too much.

Grandfather looked at me and nodded, as if he knew what I was thinking.

Aiden helped me pack up my books while my mother picked through my clothes. Eventually, she pronounced most of them unsuitable and left them hanging in the closet.

"We'll go shopping," Mom said running her fingers over my sleek straight black hair. It had been pink and spiky before this so-called hospital. "Tamarind Bay has shops that rival Tokyo."

On my way out, I found my Sasuke-san sitting slumped at the table in the garden, staring into his cold cup of tea. The scene looked oddly familiar. The hummingbirds flittered in my brain as I kissed him on the forehead.

"We got them back," I whispered.

1:28 AM. SOMEWHERE IN THE CITY OF HAMILTON . . .

Good morning, citizens. Our dear mayor has proclaimed that his ID program will make us all safer, that it could make the whole country—maybe even the whole world— safer. And he's going to ride that idea—and a boatload of TFC money—right into Congress. His sponsors love him. The press eats up every word. He's got a slew of other Patriot Party candidates and legislators on his bandwagon.

However, nobody seems to be asking him the big question. How exactly does an ID in your skull make you safe? The TFC-partiers say it's unpatriotic to ask.

But I'm asking.

Sure, the chip would be a great Lo Jack for missing kids, deadbeat dads, and cheating spouses. The cops already track felons this way. But wouldn't a smart terrorist (or other criminal) just get the ID? Or a fake one? You know they're going to pop up on the black market sooner rather than later.

So ask yourself why this ID chip is suddenly a requirement. Why did TFC insist that Nomura bring out the chip (and their new mobiles) now instead of in the fall as planned? Who gains?

Next up for your listening pleasure, "Follow the Money" by Political Business. And then we've got "Wait until July Comes" by a local band who wishes to remain anonymous.

9.0

BAGGED, TAGGED, AND RELEASED

VELVET

Somebody did need to do some explaining, but I didn't know who that somebody was.

The cops? Hardly. Spike? A fat lot of good that'd do. Dad? I hated to worry him about stuff at home. Mom? Maybe. I live in hope.

It started to rain. How cliché.

Do not run. *Book of Velvet*. Chapter 3, Verse 12. Not from or toward anything.

My boots slapped the wet pavement as I walked past boarded-up houses. Spike lives on the nicer end of the West End. Mom and I rent the bottom of a sad-looking triplex on the crappier end. The top floors of our once pretty Victorian were empty. We'd pried off the plywood from the second-floor windows so that people wouldn't assume the whole place was vacant—and thus up for grabs in the squatting department.

By the time I hit my front door, I was feeling like a stunned (and drenched) animal who'd been tranq'ed and released back into the wild.

Bagged, tagged, and released. With no idea who the baggers were.

"Is that you, Anne Marie?" Mom yelled from the kitchen. A pack of mongrels from Chihuahua up to mastiff-size bounded out to greet me. One of Mom's causes. "Don't let the new pups out."

I knew the drill. This wasn't my first dog rodeo. But a new dog, a big black one that kind of looked like the dog on the Black Dog Architectural sign, blocked the door into the kitchen. I stood my ground but didn't make eye contact.

"She's okay, Bridget," Mom said evenly.

The dog sniffed me and stepped aside, her tail wagging slowly.

"That one is very protective." Mom was busy sorting out the garbage and putting the organic stuff in the composter. "How many times have I told you, Anne Marie, to put your coffee grounds and table scraps into the compost?"

"Mom, we don't even have a garden." *We could just use a disposal like everyone else.*

"It's on my list."

Mom has a long list of projects—and causes. She actually takes the compost to the community plot to trade for fresh veggies. She's the queen of bartering.

"Mom?" I grabbed a towel from the laundry basket and dried myself off.

The new black dog nudged Mom for a bit of stinky cheese she was throwing in the compost. "Such a sad story." Mom tsked. She grabbed the dog a biscuit from the treat jar as she talked. "She was—"

"Mom," I cut her off. They're all sad stories. The animal shelter. The people shelter. Whatever I have to complain about just doesn't compare. Usually. "When did I get this ID chip behind my ear?"

"Honey, you know how I feel about those things. But if you want one, I'm not going to stop you." She'd moved on from compost to feeding the dogs. She doled out the kibble into six dishes and mediated a squabble between two of the puppies.

Mom is against *things*. She grudgingly carries a mobile. We have a screen, but she keeps it covered up with a pretty fair-trade cotton cloth from a swap meet. She is in technology denial.

I tossed the towel onto the dirty laundry pile and then sealed up the compost bucket she'd left open.

"No," I said. "I already have one, but I don't remember getting it."

"Oh, thank you, hon." Mom took the bucket by the handle and wrestled it out into the backyard, placing it next to four other buckets. No doubt it was on her list to get those buckets down to the community garden. Right after she found homes for all the dogs, worked her shift in the food pantry, clothed all the homeless in Hamilton, sent books to all the soldiers in Syria, built a new wing on the Toys'R'Us children's cancer ward, and generally solved world peace. "So what did you say? You got an ID chip? Well, you needed one for school, anyway, so it's fine with me."

I gave up. I wasn't on her list.

At least it had stopped raining.

She pecked me on the cheek as she hurried back inside. "I've got to get cleaned up for the spouses' meeting. Mr. Severin found out his wife was killed in Damascus, and his son isn't coping very well. Can you make your own dinner? I may be back late," she called through the kitchen window. She didn't wait for my answer.

I wish Winter were here.

The dogs were eating happily when I stepped back into the kitchen. I stared at the contents of the fridge. A wad of lettuce. Two shriveled carrots. A green pepper. Tofu. Four jars of mayo. A loaf of white bread. Half a can of tuna. All were either from the community garden or the food bank, where she volunteered.

What I wouldn't give for a cheeseburger.

While Mom was in the shower, I grabbed the leather-bound notebook Dad had sent me for my last birthday and a pack of smokes, both of which I keep under my mattress, and went out to the backyard. I dried off the old Adirondack chair Mom had found kicked to the curb. She'd repainted it sage green, but the chair still listed to one side. I wedged it between the apple tree and the fence to keep from toppling over.

Such is my life.

I played a music 'cast on my mobile and stared at a blank page in my notebook. I could tell it how I felt, but I didn't know where to begin with this one. I'd started writing some poems and lyrics earlier this year for a school project. Just bits and pieces, but I got into it.

I flipped through my notebook and read some stuff to get me in the writing mood. I started with my most recent song (unfinished, of course):

> *Money doesn't buy you happiness*
> *They say.*
> *But I'd trade my life for yours*
> *Any day.*
>
> *You've got the perfect family*
> *2.3 children and a dog*
> *All piled into a Bradley*
> *Safe behind the fog (?)*

Okay, it was crap. Fog didn't make any sense.

I turned back a few more pages. There, I'd jotted down a snippet of poetry Meme Girl read late one night:

> *...of course there's something wrong*
> *in wanting to silence any song.*
> *—"A Minor Bird" by Robert Frost*

I flipped back a few more pages and came across the chorus of another unfinished song:

> We'll remember until
> They make us forget,
> Nora.

Whoa. *Nora? Make us forget?* I snapped the notebook closed.

I did NOT remember writing those words at all.

Fumbling with a smoke, I listened to the cicadas whir above my head. A whiff of grilled meat wafted over the fence.

I miss Dad.

The 'cast reminded me that the Chipster was coming out in July, and it was like nothing I'd ever experienced. It was unforgettable.

Hah.

But. Inexplicably I wanted one. And I even felt the urge to vote. For Mayor Mignon. Weird.

The 'cast crackled, and the voice of the MemeCast trickled in like rain.

Make sure the voices in your head are your own, she said.

I scribbled that shit down.

10.0

REVENGE OF THE MONEY CATS

WINTER

Pink and lime green. And a Money Cat comforter with matching curtains. It was as if my parents had picked up my old bedroom—which we'd decorated when I was, I don't know, eight—and plopped it here in this new house. Like the last three years hadn't happened at all. At twelve, I replaced the smiling, waving Money Cats. I'd dyed the curtains and bedspread myself. Black. I was grounded for a week, but the Money Cats stayed gone. Until now.

The closet was worse. I had school uniforms hanging in there: a navy blazer with the Tamarind Bay Day School crest on the pocket, several plaid skirts, and many, many white shirts, some button up, some golf. I could see several green and navy sweaters neatly folded on the shelf. It was all very Japanese schoolgirl.

The hummingbirds fluttered.

The rest of the clothes in the closet were definitely

all Mom, though Dad probably picked out the Winnie-the-Pooh sweatshirt. It was never going to touch my body.

I swiped the darkest T-shirt and plainest jeans (no sparkly pockets) to change into, grabbed the hair wax from my bag, and headed toward the shower. At least I could fix my hair. This slick bowl cut was way too glossy.

•   •   •

Mom does this thing with her lips when she doesn't like something. She did it when I walked into the kitchen. She hated the spikes, but I felt more like me.

"Dad had to go back into work, but I took the day off to get you settled." She caught herself doing the lip thing and forced a smile.

Then we stared at each other with this okay-now-what look on our faces. We were strangers thrown into a house together, like some stupid reality 'cast. The house was nice. Very suburban. Everything spotless and carefully neutral. You could even smell how new it was.

"Okay, then," Mom said with a fake burst of energy. "Are you hungry? I can heat something up or we can go out." She said this last part looking at my spikes, as if she hoped I wouldn't pick that option.

I was tempted to say yes, let's go out. Instead, I shrugged. "Whatever."

Mom laughed. "My god, you are a teenager. It's going to take me a while to get used to it."

"I'll go easy on you. Today."

"Where have the years gone?" she asked without a bit of irony.

Tell me about it.

Again the silence. Except the hummingbirds flittered in the distance. I shook my head.

I slouched onto a bar stool at the kitchen counter. Mom opened a few cupboards and then stared into the depths of the fridge. After a moment, she announced, "I guess we need to go out." She put on her forced smile again. "And we can do a little shopping."

I am not Mall Girl. I can barely stand going to the vintage shops with Velvet. At least the stuff she thrusts at me doesn't have bears on it, not even to be ironic. Velvet doesn't get irony. Thankfully.

I should call her and Micah and let them know I'm out of the loony bin.

The hummingbirds were closer now.

Mom was looking at me like I was supposed to say something. Oh yeah. Shopping. Mall.

"Okay," I said. I didn't have the heart to get all teenager on her again. Besides, I haven't seen her in three years. Not that I remember, at least.

We took the Skyway to the Hub, the center of the compound, where the schools, shops, and offices are. I tried to call Micah and Velvet on the way, but neither call went through. Blocked.

Mom's doing, I'm sure.

The Sky, as most people call it, is a walkway like

the one in Hong Kong: a series of multilevel, moving and stationary walkways linking the residential areas of the compound with the Hub. The Sky is actually a genius bit of engineering—marred only by the ads and stock tickers projected along the sides. Green Zone. ExxonMobilShell. TFC. Mega-Gap. Nomura.

Mom pointed out my school and the exit I needed to take as we passed over it. She prattled on about how this school is better than the one on the other side of the Hub, which is mostly performing arts oriented. My school is more academically rigorous, she said. Translation: mathletes and pre-law. She told me about Tamarind Day's engineering program, the students who went on to MIT, the five Rhodes Scholars, and so on. She also talked about the Bay's nonexistent crime rate, the parks, the shopping. She was a regular tour guide.

Finally I said, "Mom, I need coffee." I steered her toward a Starbucks on the mezzanine level of the mall. I ordered a double espresso.

"How long have you been drinking coffee?" she asked as we sat down at a table overlooking the Sky.

"Years." I took a long sip. I could feel the warm sugary goodness beginning to flow through my veins. Mom watched me closely, as if searching for something familiar to hold on to. "Tell me about Japan," I said, trying to get a conversation going. "What was Tokyo like?"

"Oh, it was very clean. Crowded, of course. Great shopping." She took a sip of her tea. "We spent most of our time working, though. Developing the new product line. Testing new components. Usual stuff."

Could her answer be any more generic? The hummingbirds buzzed in my ear.

"Did you do anything fun? Did you go to the museums? Mount Fuji? Sing karaoke?" I wasn't sure why I needed to know this. I guess I wanted to be able to picture what she'd been doing for the last three years, what was more important than being here with me.

Mom blinked at me. "I'm sure we did, but that doesn't matter now. We're home. Everything is okay. We can get on with our lives. Forget about the past. You need to work hard. Go to school. A good school. Work for the company."

It was my turn to blink at her. The hummingbirds fluttered in my head, but that little voice, the one that had told me about the hospital and Japan, was quiet.

And it was now inside my mother's head.

NOT THE RIGHT QUESTIONS

WINTER

Mom dragged me around to a few high-end shops at the Hub. I wasn't into it. I kept asking her about Tokyo. And I kept getting the same robotic responses—until she became irritated and told me to drop it. Then she changed the subject back to me.

She ended up grilling me about all the little details of my life in the last three years. How was I doing in school? Who were my friends? Did I like anybody special? I shrugged a lot.

She wasn't really asking the right questions.

• • •

The next day, Mom suddenly had so much to do at the office. She asked if I minded being left on my own.

"That's fine," I said. *More than fine.*

But after she left, I realized there wasn't much to do in our squeaky-clean, all-new house. I could watch 'casts or read. I flicked through a few 'casts on the big screen—news mostly. A rash of car bombings in Philly. *Hamilton's ID program will save us from Philly's fate*, some random guy said. Our mayor, Albert Mignon, chided those who hadn't complied yet. *Your procrastination may jeopardize the safety and security of your community*, he said with an icy smile. The Canadians were protesting the new wall across the border. Same old crap.

I couldn't sit still. Never could. I needed something to do, but there was zero tinkering material in the house. No tools. No found objects. Nothing interesting to take apart. Sure, I could disassemble the fancy pasta maker or vacuum cleaner that looked like it had never been used. But I like my found objects to be more *found*. As in rescued from the trash, swapped for at meetups, or bartered for on the Hour Exchange.

Micah is a good source. He lives in a salvage yard and helps the owner reclaim old houses. He'd bring me bits of rusted iron, busted clocks, smashed electronics—the stuff that couldn't be fixed up and resold. It was the perfect shit to bang into sculptures.

Or I'd go down by the railroad tracks to the old transportation museum scrapyard. All the cool stuff that was once in the museum downtown—rockets, trains, satellites, old cars—ended up on the scrap heap after the museum was sold to Security Home Depot, who'd turned the building into expensive, high-security lofts. Someone was always hanging around the yard making something interesting out of old train parts, ancient printers, and the odd solar panel. That's where Micah and I met, at one of Big Steven's welding workshops. And that guy, Roger, who taught underground networking, knew his shit so well he went white hat not too long ago.

I needed to get out, but I was restricted to Tamarind Bay for the duration. However long that was. Until I was deemed sane enough, I guess, to be trusted in the outside world.

So I was off to the Hub again. I checked the directory on my mobile as I rode the Sky into the Hub. Nope. There wasn't a single junk shop or thrift store in all of Tamarind Bay. But I'd seen a craft store and a gadget place that might have something I could work with.

The craft store was a bust. It mostly sold cheap art supplies, party balloons, and gift baskets. I did get some pliers and copper wire from the jewelry-making section, though. So not a total bust.

The gadget store was better. It at least had programmable building blocks and replacement remotes. I didn't know what I was going to do with them, but I felt better having something.

I picked up a Bento Box from Ben Maki's Sushi and sat out in the open-air court near the Sky platform. I shoved shrimp *nigiri* into my mouth as I looked up info on Tokyo on my mobile.

Mom said they'd lived in Shibuya Ward near the Nomura headquarters. Shibuya was not only the home of the IT industry in Tokyo, the guide said, it was also the hip district for young people. Shibuya's fashion and nightlife were famous. It's where the Japanese schoolgirl culture started in the 1990s. I saw pictures of big-haired blonde Japanese girls wearing plaid school uniforms—too much like the ones in my closet—and tons of makeup. They almost looked like dolls. Thank goodness the look had nearly died out.

The guide said there were dozens of museums in Tokyo, including the Matori Contemporary Art Museum near Shibuya Station. I flipped through the exhibits. I almost wished I'd gone with my folks. Last year the museum had this exhibition of robotic sculptures that looked extremely cool. Anya Reismuller was the artist. An Austrian engineer-turned-artist. She used to work at Nomura.

From what I could tell, she was doing some fascinating things with self-replicating machines. They're machines that can build copies of themselves out of raw materials around them. You could send one to Mars, and the machine would build copies out of ore it mined on the planet's surface. In theory. Reismuller's sculptures built themselves out of interesting materials, like beer cans and flip-flops. The coolest one built copies of itself—out of itself. The process kept repeating—

"Nice hair," said a girl with perfectly smooth, exactingly trimmed hair. She was standing in front of my table.

A gaggle of equally polished girls stood by the Sky platform. Not a spiked hair or old piece of clothing in the bunch.

I held up a finger and took a moment to finish what I was reading on my mobile.

It wasn't like the scene had never played out before. We had girls in my old school that made themselves feel better by running down anyone different. Velvet had taught me how to play these things. I finished the article and slid my mobile shut.

"I'm sorry. You were saying something?" I looked up. Eye contact and confidence were key, according to Velvet.

"Nice hair," the girl said again with less certainty.

I stared at her for a few seconds. I really wanted to say something like "my poor blind grandmother worked really hard on it this morning. Then she died." But master Velvet always said to never give them anything to latch on to. Be smooth, glassy, and hard. *Book of Velvet.* Chapter 23, Verse 3000.

"Thanks," I said as glossily as I could. "Is there anything else? No? Cool." I didn't wait for her reply. I went back to reading about Reismuller's new exhibition in Singapore.

"Freak," the girl said as she turned to shoo her crowd toward the fro-yo shop. I could hear more whispering and giggling, but I wouldn't give them the satisfaction of looking up. Act like you barely notice them. That's what they want. Attention.

I should call Velvet.

"Ladies," I heard someone say, followed by a new round of whispering and giggling.

I snuck a peek to see Aiden passing by the girls. The leader girl stepped toward him as she threw a superior look my way. I heard another one say something to her pal about Aiden inheriting Nomura North America some day.

"You're looking glossy today." He flashed a very charming, boarding school smile at the pack leader—and kept on walking toward me. Leader girl threw me an icy look.

I tried hard not to laugh.

Aiden flipped around the chair in front of me and straddled it backward. "Win-chan, did you tell these charming young automatons to go eff themselves?"

I smiled.

"Did you know that there's a Skywalk in Tokyo, too?" I asked.

"What are you reading?"

"Just a little research about Tokyo. Mom and Dad were there for three years and apparently did absolutely nothing. Work, shop, sleep."

He scooted his chair closer so he could peer at my mobile screen. I showed him some of the cool things I'd found, like the Reismuller exhibit.

"Have you been to Japan?" I asked him.

"Not since I was maybe five or six. I remember riding a very fast train into this huge station. Mom and I got lost. When we finally emerged outside, we were in a sea of people all trying to cross the street at once."

"That must have been Shibuya Station." I showed him a pic of the massive pedestrian crossing out front.

"Yeah. I'd never seen so many people. And there were older kids dressed like old-timey rock stars. Oh, I remember a dog statue."

I scrolled through another few pics until I got to Hachiko, the dog immortalized outside the station.

"On the train, Mom told me the story about how the dog waited faithfully every day at the station for his master to come home. Except one day, he didn't get off the train—the master, that is. He died. The dog kept waiting for him—until he died. The dog's body is in a museum nearby. Mom wouldn't take me to see the body."

I had a far better picture of Japan from Aiden's sketchy six-year-old memory than I'd gotten from two grown people who'd lived in the city for three years. Something didn't add up.

"How was Switzerland?" I asked. Aiden had been there the same length of time my parents had been in Japan.

"Oh, I worked. I shopped. Didn't see a thing."

"Shut up," I said, laughing.

"School was okay. Bern's a beautiful place—if you like Gothic cathedrals and medieval castles and snowcapped Alps—but it's kinda boring compared to Zurich. Not too much to do on the weekends except study and ski and drink." Aiden described the clock tower, a sculpture he'd seen in Lucerne that reminded him of my garden, plus a few places he'd explored. Underground tunnels. Crypts.

Clock towers. The whole hacker, adventurer, rattle-on-doors thing he loves.

Then we talked about Tamarind Bay, the school here, and how I was going to miss my friends and my grand-father. I didn't mention Jet. She's the lead tattoo artist at Grandfather's main shop downtown. I have a crush on her.

"I don't think I'll really miss anyone—except my mom. And maybe she'll come to the States more often now." Aiden's voice sounded far away.

"Do you remember when my parents left for Japan?"

"No, not really. I think I was already at Bern Academy by then."

"I remember that now. It was about a week or so before my parents disapp—went away. Right in the middle of a semester."

"Mom said she wanted me close to her for a while. I thought it meant they were getting divorced or something. The next thing I heard was that you were at Mr. Yamada's. Mom said not to bring up your folks' trip if I talked to you, because you were really freaked out about it. And you never brought it up."

"Why don't I remember them leaving or ever calling or visiting?"

"My dad hardly ever called me. Do you think your grandfather took you to TFC after they left?"

I shook my head. It sounded plausible, but Grandfather hates TFC. He always says that memories, good or bad, are part of who we are. Besides, I had other memories that didn't quite fit with that explanation. "I remember being angry and scared about them being gone. But I wasn't mad at them. And I remember Grandfather hiring lawyers and going to court to get them out of the Big D." I said the last part quietly.

Aiden's face looked like there was a tug-of-war going on in his brain.

"Okay, give. What did they tell you about me?"

"Truth? Mom said you were having paranoid delusions about your parents being gone. Crazy shit about the government taking them. That's why you went to the hospital. That's why Uncle Brian and Aunt Spring came home."

And why Aiden came home.

Maybe I was crazy, but the whole Japan thing didn't add up.

I needed to hear it from Mom and Dad. I needed to hear it from my Sasuke-san, but Mom was still too mad at him to let me talk to him. Or any of my friends, for that matter. Micah would know if I was crazy. Velvet would, too, but this is more the kind of thing I would have told Micah. He does serious better than Velvet. But someone had blocked my calls to anyone who might have been able to back me up. So Mom and Dad would have to do.

Aiden caught my hand as I pushed away from the table. "Winter, why did you send me that book?" he asked in a hushed tone.

That snapped me out my spiraling thoughts.

"What book? I don't remember sending you anything."

Aiden glanced at the security cams hanging over the food court. I hadn't really noticed them before.

"Come to the car with me," he whispered. "I'll give you a ride home," he added more loudly.

The hummingbirds fluttered in my brain.

AN ENIGMA WRAPPED IN A LIBRARY BOOK

AIDEN

"You're as bad as Micah," Winter said as we walked through the security checkpoint into the parking garage. "Paranoid," she clarified when I raised my eyebrow Dad-style.

Maybe she was right, but I couldn't take the chance that the security cams would pick us up.

The universe muttered its agreement as a camera swiveled and followed us to the waiting car.

We slipped into the back of the limo, and I flicked on the privacy screen between us and Jao before taking out the book.

"Nice." Winter grabbed the book from my hands. It was a book on kinetic sculpture, after all. She flipped through the first few pages, devouring the pictures as if she'd never seen them before.

"I sent you this?" she asked.

"Keep going," I told her.

She flipped through a few more pages before she gasped. She'd found the secret stash.

"Recognize them?"

She pulled out the *Memento*s and studied them. "No," she said. She pressed one of the pages to her nose and inhaled. "Uh, I don't think so, at least."

But I could see she was scanning that hard-drive brain of hers, looking for some lost bit of data. I could almost hear the clicking.

"The work definitely looks like Micah's, though," Winter finally said.

She reminded me that Micah is her homeless skater friend who draws. And who is evidently paranoid. Maybe rightly so.

"He's good," I said.

She nodded, flipping through the comics again. "These must be new. I don't remember them, and he shows me everything. I mean *everything*."

"But you sent them to me." I said it slowly so it would sink in.

She shrugged helplessly. "Sorry." She pulled out her mobile and showed me a pic of a curly-headed kid with glasses and a scruffy goatee. Micah Wallenberg, her contact list said. "His number is blocked on my mobile. Same with Velvet and the rest of my friends." She sounded angry now. Aunt Spring must have done that in her motherly zeal to keep Winter safe. From what, I don't know.

"Let me try." I spoke Micah's name and number into my mobile. I got a weird message saying this person was unavailable.

Then I tried Velvet. It connected, and I handed my mobile to Winter.

"Velvet? I'm so glad to hear your voice! My mobile's blocked. Hmm? This is Aiden's. You know, my cousin. I'm okay. No, I'm restricted to the compound—" They chatted for several minutes at an even higher rate of speed. Then Winter abruptly handed the mobile back to me. "She wants to talk to you."

It wasn't much of a two-way conversation. I did a lot of agreeing, including agreeing to come by the store where she worked so I could tell her in person how Winter really was.

That was fine with me. I had some things I wanted to ask her.

13.0

WAITING FOR THE BRAVE NEW WORLD TO CHANGE

VELVET

Huxley's was deader than usual—and I really couldn't afford to keep recycling my paycheck through the shop's antiquated till. Mrs. Huxley is against a lot of the same things as my mom—like gridded technology. They're friends. And, yes, that's how I got the job.

Still, I had nothing better to do than browse the new vintage jackets and play dress-up until Winter's cousin got here or a customer popped in. The latter wasn't likely at this time of day. "Business" would pick up later after we closed, during the unspoken, unadvertised Hour Exchange hours. Mrs. H. worked those herself.

I didn't like deciding on barters, anyway. How many dresses does four hours of free legal service or five loaves of French bread equal? Only Mrs. H. could judge that.

"Nothing Ever Happens" by the Lo-Fi Strangers roared

over the store's old-fashioned stereo system, while I slipped on a black leather jacket. I modeled it with my current ensemble. Too biker chick.

Spike called while I was trying on the vintage Chanel suit with my black lace tights.

Ignore. Don't talk to fools when you're still mad at them. Or yourself. *Book of Velvet*. Yada, yada, yada.

I was modeling the peasant skirt with combat boots when Aiden came in. The effect was sort of punk little-house-on-the-prairie. Not my best work.

"Velvet?" he asked. I could feel him staring, but I didn't give him the satisfaction of looking at him.

I held up my hand. "I'll be right with you." I ducked into the dressing room again and changed back into my jeans.

Now it was my turn to stare.

Aiden Nomura looked like he'd stepped out of a J.Crew catalog. Not bad on the eyes, but nothing like Winter. If I hadn't been expecting him, I would've directed him to the mega-Gap three blocks away.

"I'm Aiden." He reached out his hand and launched into this full-charm initiative, with just the right smile and tilt of his head. "Nice shop—"

I put the counter between us.

He kept talking some crap about liking the store, yada, yada, yada. I stopped listening. Never listen to BS wrapped in a polo shirt and $300 shoes. Finally, he came up for air.

"You're Winter's cousin?" I let the incredulity sink in.

"Um, yeah," he said, put off his game, whatever it was.

"Velvet Kowalcyk," I said. I made a show of appraising his outfit.

"What is it with you and Winter?" He chuckled. "I have to look the part, you know."

I guess we all do. Corporate prince. Wannabe rock star. Vintage store screw-up. Everybody except maybe Winter. She doesn't care.

"How is our girl? Really," I asked.

"That's what I'm trying to figure out," he said earnestly. The Prince Charming façade fell away like an ill-fitting prom dress.

Now I could see the resemblance. In the eyes. He had Winter's intensity.

Aiden Nomura slung his backpack on the counter and glanced around before he pulled out a large coffee-table art book. "She doesn't remember sending me these." He slipped out a set of cartoons—which were obviously drawn by Micah. No doubt.

Winter (and Micah) always had art books like this around, but I didn't remember seeing the comics—and I think I would because they were disturbingly good.

"Definitely Micah's," I said to Aiden's unasked question.

"We got a weird message when we called him."

I put the drawings back into their hidey hole and closed up the book tightly. Aiden watched.

"Micah's in juvie." *And now I know why.*

"When did that happen?" Aiden shoved the book into his pack.

"Right before the cops raided Black Dog Village and found 'suspicious' materials there. Bomb-making stuff, they said." I explained to Aiden that BDV was a homeless village where Micah used to live. And that the raid happened in mid-May, about the time school let out. "Luckily, his mom got one of those new TFC-sponsored apartments on Norfolk Avenue right before the raid."

Whoa, whoa, whoa. Now that I'd said it out loud, I wondered: How did I know all this? I strained to remember. I hadn't talked to his mom. Or to Winter's mom for that matter. I'd just gotten the weird messages when I called. How did I know about the hospital? And that Nora James moved to Los Palamos? Like I care about her?

"Are you okay?" Aiden asked. I hadn't noticed him coming around the counter, but there he stood, leaning against it, looking all concerned into my face.

I studied his. He seemed a lot like Winter now, in the ways that counted, only glossier on the outside. And harder to get a handle on. Could I tell him? About the chip? About what I just realized I don't remember?

Not in those clothes.

"We need to do something about all this." I waved my hand over his perfectly put together ensemble. But I really meant something else. I think.

9:42 AM. SOMEWHERE IN THE CITY OF HAMILTON . . .

Good morning, citizens. Today let's talk about things you might not hear about on Action 5—or the national Action News 'cast. Or any newscast in this country.

Yesterday the French government closed down TFCs in Paris after a riot broke out in front of a clinic near the Sorbonne. The crowd, mostly students from the university, was heard shouting "Memento!" as they turned over a black van.

A similar incident happened in Athens this morning.

French and Greek authorities are investigating.

Next up: The Silence's version of "The Revolution Will Not Be Televised."

STUCK IN A MOMENT

WINTER

Over dinner that night, which Mom ordered in from some Thai place, she and Dad talked work.

"The ID chip interface isn't going to be ready in time if Ichiro keeps micromanaging the whole project," Dad said, shoveling Pad Thai into his mouth.

"He's just stressed because the client bumped up the schedule so much."

"Well, he could trust some of us to do our jobs." Dad stabbed his chopsticks into the pile of noodles.

Mom passed the curry.

I didn't care about family or company politics (which were the same thing); I had only one thing on my mind: Japan. I was stuck on it.

"Did you guys see the Anya Reismuller exhibit at the Watari last year?" I asked.

"The what at the what?" Dad said, his mouth full.

"The Watari Museum of Contemporary Art. It's between Shibuya station and Nomura headquarters. The artist does these amazing robotic sculptures."

Dad shook his head as if I'd suggested they might have gone deep-sea diving for sponges or something. Dad's idea of art is an engineering blueprint or a fast car. He likes things that do what they're supposed to do—well.

"No, I'm afraid we didn't, dear," Mom said. She writes code for a living, but her idea of art is hanging in her closet. Actually, that's not true. She doesn't really care about fashion; she just wants to fit in.

"The artist used to work for the company. I thought maybe you would've gone to support her. A little company loyalty. Like Hachiko."

"Who?" Mom asked.

"You know, the famous dog statue right outside the train station you used every day for the past three years."

"Enough." Dad slammed his chopsticks on the table. Mom was beginning to tear up.

I'd struck something here.

"Can't you just leave it alone?" he asked.

"No." I stared at my dad, looking for that missing piece of the puzzle rattling around in his brain. "I don't think you were in Tokyo at all."

"What? You think because we don't know some touristy stuff you looked up online that we weren't really in Japan?"

He had me there. I shook my head. "No, but something just doesn't make sense."

"Look, Winnie," Mom said. I cringed at the name. "Our memory is a little hazy because of a special project we worked on there. One Ichiro didn't want leaked. So—"

"So you brain-bleached yourself?" That was just as crazy as what I had been thinking. "Okay, so then why don't I remember you going to Japan in the first place? Or you ever calling me in three years? And don't say Grandfather TFC'd me. He'd never."

Mom glared at me, but I wouldn't let it go.

"And why did he spend all that time and money on lawyers to get you out of Detention?" I'd said it. The D word. They were in the Big D, not the Big J.

"Oh, Winnie." My father sighed and looked at Mom, who was crying now. "Look what you've done."

"Honey, I'm sure your grandfather was having his own legal problems." Mom sniffed. "I hope he wasn't contributing to your—"

"Delusions?" I finished for her. "I'd like to hear all this from him."

"That's not a good idea. We're making an appointment for you with the doctor Ichiro recommended."

"Winnie," my dad said. "We're home. Everything is okay. We can get on with our lives. Forget about the past. You need to work hard. Go to school. A good school. Work for the company."

Where had I heard that before?

15.0

BREAKFAST IN AMERICA

AIDEN

The clock blinked seven AM at me, and for a brief sleepy moment, I wondered why on Earth I'd set the alarm. It was way too early for summer. Then it came to me.

My internship started today. Groan.

I rolled out of bed.

The skinny black jeans and red pseudo-western shirt Velvet had picked out for me hung over the closet door. I hoped she was kidding.

Mom called while I was in the shower to tell me to behave myself at the office.

I ought to wear this cowboy punkware to work.

I didn't.

White shirt. Check. Khakis. Check. Tie. Check.

Dad was eating breakfast when I came downstairs. I

suspected he'd waited to make sure I was actually pre-sentable and on time.

He gave me one of his arched eyebrow looks but didn't say anything. He just dipped his *tamagoyaki*—a rolled omelet—in soy sauce and motioned for me to sit. Cook had made a traditional Japanese breakfast for us. Rice. Broiled Salmon. *Tamagoyaki*. Miso. Something pickled. Tea.

I'm usually a caffeine and sugar guy. School always had Müesli for breakfast, but there was a bakery nearby that made amazing fried apple-bread things and coffee. It was worth being late for class.

"Cook can prepare something else, if you wish."

"No, this is okay." I could run to Starbucks later. No need to get off on the wrong foot with the old man.

I broke off a piece of fish with my chopsticks and shoveled it in my mouth with some rice. The salty mouth-ful of goodness surprised me. It was like coming home—to a home I'd forgotten about. I still intended to get a latte later, though.

Dad smiled as I polished off the salmon. And the rice. He waited until I sipped the miso to say something.

"You'll be working in the testing lab this summer with Roger Nyugen." He allowed Cook to clear away his plates. "He's a good kid. You two have a lot in common."

I raised one of my eyebrows, and Dad let out a small chuckle.

"Yes, he's been in trouble, but he's turned himself

around. For his family." Dad explained that Roger was supporting his younger brother while his parents were in Saigon on business. The company, meaning Dad, was going to give Roger a scholarship for school this fall. "It's a surprise, so don't mention it."

I sipped my tea. I saw where this was going. Roger was supposed to be the good example for me to follow, my mentor on the road to the straight and narrow.

"Don't worry, there will be plenty of interesting doors for you to crack open." Dad must've sensed I wasn't buying the kid-from-the-streets sob story angle. "We have a new version of the Chipster set to ship in a few weeks. They were supposed to release this fall, but our client wants to release its new Chipster app early. We haven't even finished testing everything."

Product testing was usually done months ahead of release, and Dad is a notorious control freak. *No wonder he let me come home. Free labor.*

"Do they want it in time for SecureCon?" That was a big industry conference traditionally held over Fourth of July weekend.

Dad nodded. "The new TFC app is due out July first, and they've invested a lot in our partnership."

"TFC?" I asked, recalling the ad I'd seen on the plane. *It'll be like having a TFC right in your pocket.* "Really?"

Dad had always said that TFC was unethical and manipulative, and that he'd never do business with them.

"Sometimes you have to protect your interests," he said quietly.

And your interests are money. Not ethics. Not family. Money.

Dad rose. "I have a meeting." On his way out the door, he added quietly, "I missed you."

I think he actually meant it.

16.0

EATING THE DOG FOOD

AIDEN

Aunt Spring met me in the lobby of Nomura's Research and Development Division. Sans Winter.

"She's not quite ready to work yet, Aiden," Spring said. "She needs to settle in."

She handed me my ID badge, which she explained was mostly for visual reassurance. Translation: the other employees would know I belonged there. All secure trans-actions—that is, getting into the building and most areas inside—were handled by biometric scans. She led me to the Product Testing Department but stopped with a hand on the door.

"When Winter is ready to come in—even before—would you mind keeping an eye on her?"

"Of course not." *That's why I came home.*

Aunt Spring turned me over to one of the product

testing geeks, Roger Nguyen—my supposed mentor. He was maybe eighteen, if that, with fidgety, scarred hands and intense eyes. He struck me as the male version of Winter, minus the artistic genius. Roger handed me a testing protocol to read and disappeared into his cubicle.

My eyes glazed over as soon as I hit the second paragraph. The protocol was forty pages long.

Roger came back twenty minutes later with two cups of coffee and a handful of sugar packets. I was reading the product reports I'd downloaded to my mobile.

"Look, I know you're the Big Kahuna's son, but you gotta follow the protocols." He slid a Nomura mug toward me.

His own well-worn cup had a faded penguin in a tuxedo on the side. The bird was the symbol of a company that promoted open source code. Once upon a time, programmers thought you should be able to share code, collaborate, and build new and wonderful things together. For free. The cup was ancient—if it was real. Roger was using it to establish his geek street cred.

I could play that game. "Dude, I've been eating the dog food since I was weaned." I slapped my Nomura Chipster pre-beta on the desk.

Roger almost did a spit-take with his coffee. In the software-hardware world, dog food equaled product, whatever product the company made. There was an old saying: it's good to eat your own dog food. That is, you consume (read: test) what you make. Dad always had me testing shit.

Roger flipped over my phone to read the Kanji on the back. "You have the beta of the model that's being released soon." He slapped another mobile on the table. "Want the beta of version 2.0? It was supposed to roll out this fall, but now we've got to release it this summer."

"Sure." I snatched the mobile off the table.

"We also have betas and prerelease candidates of the Soma and a few other models to test, but their chipset is based on the Chipster's. The priority, though, is the Chipster." Roger shook his head. "Such a kludge."

"Bring 'em on," I said.

And he did with a big fat grin on his face.

He left me in my own cubicle with a pile of mobiles and a bigger pile of paperwork. Not literally paper, of course. He set up the terminal so I could fill out electronic forms as I tested.

Forms. My summer was going from geek to bleak. Still, I eyed the terminal and mobiles.

Be good, Mom's voice echoed in my head. I knew exactly what she meant. This internship was kind of like giving an alcoholic a summer job tasting wine. I was expected to taste but not swallow. Spit it out and move on to the next vintage.

I wondered what Velvet was doing this summer.

Roger's mobile buzzed in his cubicle.

He listened a moment and then let out a squirrely little laugh. "Nah, he's just a rich skid," he said seriously, and then hung up.

A skid. A script kiddie. It's what serious hackers called wannabes who ripped off other people's code or downloaded off-the-shelf scripts from Russian or Filipino boards to do the heavy lifting. Kids like me.

17.0

LATHER. RINSE. REPEAT.

AIDEN

For the next few days, I was stuck in a loop of crushing boredom. Face-time breakfast with Dad, who was clearly stressing about this July 1 deadline. Work (in which I behaved). Dinner. Hanging with Winter, who seemed more and more obsessed with her parents not having been in Japan. (I admit this had me worried about her.) Lather. Rinse. Repeat.

I needed to explore. I needed to pull on a few doors and see what the universe had for me, unearth some hidden world that nobody else knew about. A forgotten steam tunnel. A locked clock tower. An abandoned chalet. A back door to a program. (Even if I was a quote-unquote skid.)

The Hub in Tamarind Bay had nothing interesting to offer. I'd looked, hoping it was like Disney World, with its underground system for employees to get magically around. Nada.

"You have one of the new ID chips, right?" Roger asked as he handed me a batch of the newest betas that were slated for fall release.

"Mine's about four years old." I'd gotten an ID chip back when I lived in Tamarind Bay before going away to school. I didn't need one in Bern.

"These models only work if you have the nGram, but you can fake it out with this." Roger handed me a headset. "The ID chip is mounted inside."

I looked at him, surprised.

He shrugged. "I don't have one, either."

"When's the deadline?" Funny how Dad hadn't mentioned me getting one.

"July first," Roger said. "You'll be okay. There's probably some student exemption. I bet you won't need it at your fancy-schmancy boarding school." He glanced down at something on his mobile.

"I got kicked out for hacking the payroll," I said as he started walking away. "Weak, showy shit really." I needed to feel him out.

"You wanted to get caught?" Roger slowed, looking back at me. "And your dad put you here?" Roger seemed amused.

"I've been a good little white hat. So far." I sighed. "I'll find something else to challenge myself with."

Roger rolled his eyes and then left me alone. He was far more interested in his mobile.

Not quite the reaction I was going for.

I was hoping he'd ask "like what?" And then I'd bring up *Memento*. Somehow.

Screw him. I'd figure this *Memento* thing out on my own.

Problem was, I was stuck. GIGO. Garbage in, garbage out.

Micah was a wash—at least until he got out of juvie, and even then he might not remember. Should I find Nora? She probably didn't remember a thing, either.

Then the universe gave me a big, fat hint.

The test mobile picked up a crackle and then the sound of a woman's voice.

This is the MemeCast. All that you remember may not be the truth.

TIME TO GO OLD SCHOOL

AIDEN

The MemeCast lasted only a few minutes. She told the story of an older man who'd once ninjaed (her words) around the city like a superhero, but was now humbled by the horrific memory of something—a mugging—that didn't really happen to him. *My sources say a little chip might have something to do with it,* she said. Then she played a song by a local band about spitting it out, whatever "it" was, which she said was inspired by *Memento*.

She knew about *Memento*. (And what the chips were capable of.)

The 'cast was obviously unauthorized. Somebody knew what they were doing and was "broadcasting" an old-fashioned pirate radio show on the low-power spectrum. That probably meant they varied the length, timing, strength, and location of the 'cast to avoid being found.

And since nobody used these frequencies anymore, it would be hard just to stumble across the show—unless it interfered with something. Like a mobile.

Finding radio signals is pretty old-school stuff. I could drive around with a homemade directional antenna and physically hunt down the transmitter. Back in the day, I could've triangulated the signal off of radio towers. But those towers didn't work anymore. They'd been stripped, scrapped, or had fallen apart. Most people didn't even remember that radio and TV had once been broadcast over the air from towers like that—for free.

Only geeks knew that kind of stuff anymore. And only a non-skid, like my Winter, would know how to make something to track the signal.

It was time to rattle on some doors.

SOMETHING

WINTER

Finally. Something to do.

I had been so bored. I couldn't call my friends, leave the compound, or see my own grandfather. I couldn't even go into stupid work. All because Mom (and Dad, but mostly Mom) kept saying I'm still too fragile, that I need time to get my bearings.

What a load of crap.

Maybe I should stop asking them about Japan.

The hummingbirds fluttered.

Aiden described his so-called "project" and I told him what to bring. "Can I come now?" he asked.

"You'd better," I replied.

While he was here, he introduced me to the Meme-Cast.

20.0

HELLUVA FIRST DATE

VELVET

New amendment to the *Book of Velvet*: when a cute rich guy asks you to hang out, be worried if he shows up with an antenna made out of a potato chip can.

At least I dressed appropriately: old jeans, combat boots, and a Pax Victoriana tee. I was deliberately trying to look like I didn't care enough to impress him. Mission accomplished.

"What's that?" I poked my finger at the cantenna.

"We're going hunting," Aiden said. "You see, there's this pirate 'cast—"

"Yeah, the MemeCast," I interrupted.

He seemed a little miffed that I already knew about it, but it didn't put him off his explanation. Much. He wanted to find the MemeCast because the person behind it seemed to know about the *Memento*s and Winter.

Of course, I'd wondered about the 'cast, about Meme

Girl and where she got her info, but I was mostly into the music and poetry that followed her rants. I told him that. It's where I'd heard "Enough" by the Multinationals and "Minor Birds" by Robert Frost. She even played and read some local bands and poets. The conspiracy theory stuff had seemed half-baked. Until now. I rubbed the disc behind my ear.

Aiden was going on about tracking the signal.

I had to admit the idea was genius, though I wasn't going to tell him that. I had a few questions of my own that I wanted to ask. Someone. Anyone.

"Lead on, Macduff," I told him.

• • •

He did. We drove around the center of the city a bit, not talking much because he was intent on listening for the signal.

"We may not pick up anything today. She only 'casts from random locations and intervals—so people won't find her. Like this," I said.

"I'm surprised you listen to the MemeCast," he said.

I was really thinking, *Me? What about you, Mr. Richie Rich?* Instead I went with, "Don't sound so shocked. Looking good is not my only talent." I hoped he got sarcasm. Spike didn't always.

"You do look good," he said, but then quickly turned back to his signal. He rolled down the window to scan a bigger area.

"Uh, you're going to make people really nervous

ANGIE SMIBERT

driving around in a black SUV with a gun-like thing hanging out the window." We'd already gotten some panicky looks from passersby, most of whom had hustled away quickly.

He rolled the window back up. "If we could get higher . . ."

I pointed to the MLK pedestrian bridge that overlooks downtown and joins it with the West End neighborhood, where I live. "You might treat a girl to coffee on the way."

"I'll even throw in some cake." Aiden tapped on the privacy screen between us and the driver. We rolled through a drive-thru, and then Aiden told the driver where to go. It took some convincing, but the driver finally let us out at the bridge; he probably parked around the corner to keep an eye on us.

"You know," Aiden said as he swept the cantenna over the skyline. "War walking doesn't have the same romantic appeal as war driving."

This must be some usage of the word romantic that I'm not familiar with. But coffee and red velvet cake—Aiden's idea—and watching the city rush by, wasn't such a bad thing.

Aiden put down the cantenna after one last sweep and sat beside me to sip his coffee.

"How long have you known Winter?" he asked after he inhaled a slice of cake.

"Since seventh grade. She'd just moved to the

neighborhood." You could see Winter's grandfather's house from here. It was the only one with an obstacle course in the back. "She was different. I like different." We'd bonded over our distaste for physical exertion in gym glass.

"Winter didn't exactly fit in at her old school, either."

"Did you? Fit in, that is?" I asked.

"Winter got the brains; I got the charm. And I do get by on my looks." He smiled cheesily. It wasn't the multiple kilowatt Prince Charming smile he'd tried on me before. More of a parody of it. That was progress.

"How's that working for you?" I sipped my caramel latte.

"Eh. Not so much lately." Aiden snorted. He began telling me about this guy at work who seemed to have his number, too. "He thinks I'm some rich kid poser."

I didn't say a thing.

Aiden shrugged it off, but I could see it was getting under his skin. Not too many people pierced that Prince Charming armor of his.

A familiar crackle came out of the mobile he had hooked up to the antenna.

"Was that it?" I asked as Aiden scrambled for his mobile.

"There's a signal—actually a couple—but no 'cast." He scowled at his mobile. "It's coming from down there." He pointed toward a football field-sized yard of junk by the railroad tracks.

We sauntered casually over the pedestrian bridge before his driver noticed and then ran in the direction of the signal.

I knew where we were going.

THROUGH THE FUSELAGE

AIDEN

A freight train clattered by behind us as we stood at the entrance to the scrapyard. A bakery truck was parked down the block, and a rocket fuselage blocked the gate.

"This is where all the stuff from the science and trans-portation museums ended up," Velvet explained. "It's scrap now."

"It's a solid mass of junk. Rocket parts. Train cars. Old cars. Some sort of telescope thing. A section of a radio tower." I'd climbed partway up the cyclone fence to see above the rocket. "Winter would love this place."

"How do you think I know about it? I'm not Junkyard Girl." She crawled up the fence and stood on the fuselage. "Do you see a hatch?"

No. I hadn't quite pegged what girl Velvet was. Maybe that's why I liked her.

"A hatch?" she repeated. Then she stepped around me and opened a door in the rocket body that I hadn't seen.

How'd I miss that?

I jumped in after her. We hung a left in the partial darkness and crouch-walked a few dozen meters through the nose of the rocket. We emerged blinking into an open space, surrounded on two sides by walls of junk. At the far end was a white-domed building that looked like a mini-observatory.

"Are you new here?" a lanky girl in glasses asked. She'd magically appeared in front of us.

"Yes, we are." I extended my hand and moved closer to her. Time to turn on the charm. "We're doing a school project . . ."

I heard Velvet sigh heavily behind me. She thunked my antenna with her finger. I relented.

"Actually we're looking for . . ." I held out the can-tenna.

"Big Steven," Velvet finished for me.

I was going to say signal, but okay, Steven. Whoever that was. I glanced back at Velvet.

"Steve," the lanky girl bellowed. "Company." She tossed her head in the direction of the observatory.

"Big Steven?" I threw Velvet a look as we crossed the courtyard.

"He's this guy I know." Her face didn't give away a thing.

I got momentarily distracted by a pallet of old stereos,

lab equipment, printers, and whatever else was stacked against the wall of junk. "We need to come back here for our next date."

Did I really say date? Facepalm. I waited for an awkward silence to follow.

"You are so related to Winter," Velvet said without missing a beat.

Steven met us on the steps to the mini-observatory thing. Voices and laughter, mingled with static and banging, echoed inside the dome.

He was a tall, clean-cut guy, maybe nineteen or so. He could've been a former basketball player or something, but I doubt it. He was more likely an engineering student at the university. I could picture him in one of those old moon launch documentaries sitting at the mission control desk with a clipboard, a cigarette, and a cup of coffee. And a pocket protector. His barcode tattoo kind of ruined that image, though.

"Velvet? I didn't think this was your thing. Actually, I didn't think anything was your thing." He turned to me before she could respond. "And you are?"

"Aiden." I extended my hand but he left me hanging.

Velvet stepped up to Big Steven. "It is not my *thing*, Steven Michael Ambrose III." She stared him down, which was in itself quite impressive. "*Aiden's* looking for something. And he's Winter's cousin, by the way."

Steven looked at me with renewed interest. It seemed

that Winter's name had unlocked this door. Of course. This was *her* kind of place.

A sheepish grin broke out on his face and he extended his hand. "Sorry, dude, you can't be too careful nowadays. Welcome to the Rocket Garden."

Steven showed us into the dome, which probably would have been stifling hot if the canopy hadn't been cranked open.

"This thing is an old mobile observatory/tracking station from NASA. The museum got a few of them when the space program shut down. We gutted and cannibalized this one to set up our workshop."

The workshop consisted of a few folding tables, a bench loaded with power tools, some tanks for welding, buckets of circuit boards, an old vending machine, and a table saw. At one of the tables, a short-haired woman in coveralls was showing four kids how to solder. Another kid was tinkering with something across the workshop. I knew what this was.

"It's a hacker space!" I'd read about these places that provided workshops, equipment, classes—all informal—to show people how to hack or create things. The spaces sprang up every few decades, and there were some still in Europe. They weren't exactly legal in the US anymore.

"We call it a maker space. Hacker is such a touchy term."

Tell me about it. I shook my head in agreement.

"So what I've heard about you is true?" Steven asked, amused.

"What are they working on?" I said, changing the subject. I didn't really want to hear what he had to say about me—in front of Velvet.

"Becca is showing them how to make radios. Lina is packing up router kits. And over there Dune is working on a chip scanner." Steve jerked his thumb in the direction of an Asian kid, probably Vietnamese, who looked twelve or thirteen, working at a table alone.

I had to see the chip scanner.

"It looks like the one the cops use for IDs," Velvet said from across the room.

"Yes, but simpler. We don't want to read the ID, just detect if someone has one of the new ones," Dune said.

"You mean the mandatory ones?" I asked as he ran the scanner behind my ear. Nada.

"How is it that the heir apparent to the company that makes them, doesn't have a chip?" Steve asked, genuinely intrigued.

"He's been away at boarding school," Dune answered for me.

"Uh, yeah," I said staring at the kid.

"My brother works at Nomura," he said, obviously proud. "He—"

Steven cleared his throat, and Dune instantly became engrossed in the inner workings of his scanner.

Was Roger his brother? Why would Steven care if I knew?

"What's the point of scanning for a chip?" Velvet asked, derailing my thought train.

It was a good question.

Steven took the wand in his hand. "When it becomes illegal *not* to have one next week, it might be useful for those of us off the security grid to know who's really one of us."

"You never know what they plan to use the chip for, anyway," the short-haired woman in coveralls called from the workbenches. She looked familiar.

Steven ran the wand behind his own ear and another kid's. All the while Velvet was backing toward the door. What was up with that?

"Velvet?" I asked, moving in her direction.

She backed right into the lanky girl who had appeared by the door. Then Steven was in Velvet's face, running the wand behind her ear. The scanner chimed pleasantly.

"Back off," I told Steven as I came between them. "So what if she has an ID chip. It's mandatory."

I expected Velvet to rage at Steven and the others for getting in her face. I think he expected it, too. He seemed be itching for a fight for some reason. Instead, tears were running down her cheeks and she was trembling.

Steven backed off, mumbling an apology.

"Velvet," I said, touching her hands, "what is it?"

She let out a little sob. "I don't remember getting

one," she whispered. A torrent of tears and furious words spilled out of her as I held her. She shook as she told us about getting stopped by the cops. And not being able to remember the few weeks before that clearly. And how she also knew where Winter and Micah were.

I pulled her close and let her sob. Her body fit perfectly against mine, like it belonged there.

The short-haired woman brushed past us and out the door. Velvet pulled herself together, apologizing for her meltdown.

"No, I'm sorry, Velvet," Steven said. "I was just messing with you. I did not expect you to have one. Him, yes, but not you. Tell us what happened again."

She repeated her story clear-eyed but still looked pissed.

Steven paced. "I wonder if Little Steven and my parents have one."

Velvet held out her hand. "I can find out at the next band practice." She took the scanner from Steven's hand. "And by the way, he dumped me. And you're a dick."

Velvet grabbed my hand and held onto it as I led us back out through the fuselage maze into the daylight.

I never got to ask about the signal.

22.0
FLY AWAY

WINTER

I didn't want to go. Neither did the hummingbirds. The flutter of their wings grew louder and louder as our car got closer to the doctor's office. Mom gripped my hand as if I were going to fly away.

"It's up here on the left," she said more to me than to the driver. He knew where he was going: the Nomura Medical Complex.

It was a low cluster of buildings right outside the gates of Nomura North American headquarters. I'd forgotten the company preferred its own doctors. I hadn't been here since Mom and Dad went away.

Grandfather had taken me to doctors and dentists downtown. Their waiting rooms were full of old furniture, ancient magazines, and even older people.

The inside of the Nomura Medical Complex gleamed.

And we didn't have to wait. That may have been because it was Saturday.

"Dr. Ebbinghaus is ready for you, Miss Nomura." The receptionist bowed, and a crisply uniformed nurse hurried to meet us.

She whisked me away to do the whole weigh-measure-poke-prod thing in the privacy of an exam room. Through the cracked door, though, I could see Mom talking to a tall red-haired woman in a white lab coat. The woman nodded solemnly as Mom spoke. No doubt she was telling the doctor about my fixation with their so-called trip to Japan. The hummingbird wings roared in my ears. I almost missed what the doctor said when she stuck her head in the door.

"Nurse, do a quick scan. Lateral view of temporal-occipital region." She pulled the door shut behind her without even looking at me.

Something in your head, the hummingbirds said. *She wants to see something in your head.* I rubbed the raised surface of the ID chip behind my ear.

The nurse scurried around. She draped me from the neck down in a lead cloak, lowered a camera from the ceiling, carefully pointed it at my head, and then hurried out of the room. The camera made a slow circle around my head and then jerked to a stop. Nursie scurried back in and made everything disappear—cloak, camera, and herself—leaving me to stare at the blank walls and listen to the hummingbirds flitting through my head.

Well, the walls weren't entirely blank. There was a

small screen mounted in the corner, the sound muted. I could watch this wellness 'cast that seemed to be heavily punctuated by drug ads and stock reports. *I'd rather watch the walls.*

TFC's stock was up, and sure enough it was followed by an ad for some new revolutionary app promising the TFC experience over your mobile. *Forget your cares wherever you are, starting July 1st.*

Wherever you are? To do that, TFC would need to have something *inside your head.*

Shit.

I fumbled for my mobile, but I wasn't fast enough.

Everyone, including Mom, came back into the room then.

"Young lady," the doctor said to me. Her name tag said HANNAH EBBINGHAUS, MD. "You check out fine. I think we only need to adjust your medication slightly."

The nurse handed me a pill and a glass of water. The hummingbirds buzzed. Mom nodded for me to take them.

"Winnie, you need this," she said when I didn't move.

Everyone stood there, arms crossed, until I put the pill on my tongue and chased it down with the water. And then they checked to make sure I didn't spit it out.

Damn.

I told myself to call Aiden when I got to the car.

The hummingbirds grew still on the ride home. They were encased by a languid nothingness—creamy as pudding—in my head. I began to feel that everything really was going to be alright.

I could forget about the past, go to school, work for the company . . .

I needed to tell Aiden something, but I couldn't remember what.

23.0
HOME

VELVET

Aiden walked me to my door. I realized I was still holding his hand. Squeezing it, I mouthed, thanks. He touched my face where I'd been crying. This damsel thing was so not me, but I felt much better, especially as he caressed my cheek.

"We'll figure this out," he said.

Then he leaned in to kiss me. I met him halfway. He tasted like his coffee—sweet and wide awake. I probably tasted like salt. I didn't care. I just wanted to feel his arms around me again.

I pulled away slowly.

"That was a helluva first date," I said before I slipped through my front door.

Always leave them wanting more. *Book of Velvet*. Yada, yada, yada.

As great as the kiss had been, I still felt shaky and furious about what I'd let slip today.

· · ·

Mom was actually home and cooking. Not for us—but for the homeless shelter. Once a month, she scraped together enough coupons to get buttloads of free stuff or traded the coupons on the Hour Exchange for food. Then she'd make up big batches of whatever, freeze some, and donate the rest.

She was a genius at making Dad's army pay stretch around the block.

I ducked out of dinner early. It was vegan meatloaf, anyway. Whole chapters of the *Book of Velvet* are devoted to the evils of textured vegetable protein.

In my room, I turned on some tunes from my mobile, which I'd discovered quite by accident can play on my new "internal speaker." Talk about frying your cerebral cortex. (I definitely killed some brain cells with that little discovery.)

From between the mattress and box spring, I pulled out my lyric/poetry book. I scribbled down phrases and verses and refrains. I had a few complete songs, but most were in various stages of construction. Some were just ideas.

I turned to a fresh page and wrote down Steven's words, which I kept hearing in my head: *I didn't think anything was your thing*.

It pissed me off because it was true.

I'm no artist or musician or engineer. I'm not even a hacker. I can't even finish a song. My one claim to fame is the dubious ability to throw together a cheap ensemble. Big deal.

I scribbled down some more lines:

> *I may not know what song to sing*
> *Yet I could be anything*

Okay, maybe *this* could be my thing. Maybe. I'd finish this song or one of the others in my notebook, and I'd get Spike and the boys to play it. If it didn't suck.

Oh. Crap. Spike.

OUT OF FASHION, OUT OF MIND

AIDEN

I had so much to tell Winter.

Her new house was a lot like her old one. It's nice but not showy—like ours. It wouldn't be proper for Uncle Brian to have a nicer house than his older brother (and boss). Dad is very conscious of those things, even if he doesn't like to admit it.

Aunt Spring let me in. "We just got back from shopping, Aiden-kun. Come sit and have a cup of coffee. Or tea? Winter can model what she bought for us."

"Oh, that's not necessary. I'd love a cup of coffee, though."

"Nonsense, she'd be happy to do it. I'm sure she'd value your opinion."

Well, I tried. *This should be good*. For Winter to even go shopping with Spring was monumental. They don't share a passion for retail therapy—and their tastes are worlds apart.

I love my aunt, but she's always been hung up on the superficial. Maybe it's a rebellion against growing up in a tattoo shop. Maybe she wants to get out of the lab and into the boardroom. (That's Mom's theory.) Who knows.

I poured sugar and cream in my coffee and planted myself on the kitchen counter to enjoy the show.

But it wasn't the least bit funny.

Winter came out wearing a white dress with red poppies on it. It was something a twelve-year-old girl might wear to church or to the symphony. She twirled around watching the skirt wrap around her legs. She smiled at me and ran off to try something else.

She *had* to be putting us on.

"Doesn't she look lovely—and happy?" my aunt asked. The smile on her face said she didn't think Winter's performance was strange at all.

The show repeated itself a few more times. Was this performance for her mother's sake? If so, Winter had suddenly become a better bullshit artist than I was. And that was saying a lot.

Finally, Winter came out in a purple golf shirt with a bear on it and a matching plaid skirt and sneakers.

"Nice show, pumpkin," Spring said as she kissed Winter's cheek. "You kids have a nice time chatting. Winnie, remember the doctor said no caffeine." My aunt disappeared in the direction of the bedroom.

"That was a hell of a performance, *Winnie*." She hates that nickname. I waited for the placid façade to drop, for Winter to emerge and fix me with one of her looks and then rip me a new one for calling her Winnie.

It didn't happen.

She smiled at me, her eyes not really focusing. "Thanks. That's nice of you to say."

"Okay, Winter, stop shitting me."

"What? I have no idea what you're talking about." Her voice stayed very mellow.

Maybe she *didn't* know. Her pupils were huge. She swayed a bit as she stood, and one hand trembled slightly. She grabbed it and held it in front of her.

"Let's go sit out in the sun," she said, walking toward the patio.

I followed dumbly. Winter is not a sun person. I caught her when she stumbled out onto the pavers. She eased herself into a lounge chair facing the sun.

"Ah, that feels great. I could sit here all day."

She looked like she could. My Winter couldn't sit still long enough to read the directions on a shampoo bottle. Lather. Rinse. Time for a new project.

"What's going on?" I planted myself on a chair facing her.

She'd closed her eyes to soak up the sun.

"Winter?"

"Sorry." Her eyes flickered open. "This medicine makes me sleepy."

"Medicine?" Maybe she was sick, but she'd still want to know what I found out. "I saw Velvet today."

"Velvet." She knitted her eyebrows together as if she were struggling to concentrate. "She's cute, isn't she? She dresses like she's going to work in that vintage shop the rest of her life, though." She laughed. "No wonder Mom doesn't want me to talk to her. Everything is finally okay. I can get on with my life. Forget about art and humming-birds. Work hard. Go to school. A good school. Work for the company." Her eyes slid shut again, and she nodded off.

Forget about art? Work for the company? She must be stoned. My Winter would never say that sober.

The universe muttered its somber agreement.

I left Winter snoozing in the sun. Aunt Spring was in the kitchen chopping vegetables.

"Poor dear. Everything seems to take a lot out of her these days." She sounded like she was talking about her grandmother, not her fourteen-year-old daughter.

"Is it the meds?"

Aunt Spring chopped up a carrot before answering. "The delusions came back." She opened another bag of carrots and started chopping again. "You're welcome to stay for dinner," she said, looking at a mound of orange cubes in front of her.

"No, thanks, Aunt Spring. Dad expects me home." I turned to go, but then had a thought. More of an ill-formed plan. "Mind if I use the facilities first?"

"Of course not." She motioned down the hall with her knife.

I passed the guest bath and made for Winter's. Inside I found a new prescription bottle. I scanned the label with my mobile and slipped one pill into my pocket. I'm not sure why, but one of those whispers from the universe told me to seize the opportunity now.

Aunt Spring was still chopping carrots when I let myself out the front door.

11:35 PM. SOMEWHERE IN THE CITY OF HAMILTON . . .

Good evening, citizens. Today our fair city hosted a little get-together, a summit of Patriot Party leaders and hopefuls. You probably saw that on the news. Candidates big and small, all promising to make this country secure right after you vote them into office.

What you didn't see was a secret enclave of mayors from across the country meeting at TFC headquarters. My sources say they were strategizing—with TFC and Green Zone's help—about how to implement Hamilton's mandatory ID program in their own towns.

Imagine that. Chips for everyone.

This next song is "Something's Happening Here" by the Fortunate Sons.

ETERNAL SUNSHINE OF THE SPOTLESS MEMORY (CHIP)

WINTER

I woke up as the sun was setting, the heat still heavy on my brain. I'd dreamed I'd been drowning and Aiden tried to reach me, but the water had wrapped me in its arms, pulling me down into blissful nothingness. There was something I'd wanted to tell him . . .

Mom slid open the patio door. "Dinner, Winnie-chan."

I used to hate that name, but now I didn't have the energy to protest. I could smell meat and vegetables—*sukayaki*, or at least Mom's attempt at it, simmering on the stove.

I tried to get up, but at first my feet wouldn't listen. When I did get them in motion, the tremor came back in my hand.

The tremor was like the flapping of tiny bird wings as they fought to free themselves from a cage.

I didn't care.

26.0

WAY TOO MANY VARIABLES

AIDEN

I was on information overload, and the universe was no freaking help.

Dad didn't make it home for dinner. Again. Cook offered to fix me whatever I wanted, but I ordered a pizza and holed up in my room. I had to start with Winter and this latest development. I checked out the doctor and the prescription info I'd scanned off Winter's meds.

The doctor—Dr. Hannah Ebbinghaus—was a company doctor. No big surprise. Nomura had a huge medical complex for its employees. It wasn't free, of course, even though the company frowned upon you going elsewhere. But the center was supposed to be good.

I did a little searching on her name. Her specialty was cognitive disorders like Alzheimer's and Parkinson's. Was schizophrenia considered a cognitive disorder? I had no idea. Bio wasn't my subject. (Those systems had way too many variables.)

The good doctor's work seemed legitimate. Filled with altruosity even. She'd developed a memory implant to help Alzheimer's patients remember.

The drug Dr. Ebbinghaus had prescribed for Winter was an antipsychotic typically given to schizophrenics. They had too much of a neurotransmitter called dopamine in their brains. The pills blocked dopamine reception. Blah, blah, blah. Possible side effects included drowsiness and tremors, but only if the dose was too high.

It all sounded legit. The thought made me profoundly sad, though. Maybe this meant I'd never see my Winter again. Stepford Winter would replace her and live happily ever after.

The universe muttered something in the back of my brain. Sometimes you don't want to know for sure what the universe is trying to tell you.

I ate my pizza. I showered. I watched *Behind the Gates*, of all things. I could kind of see why that congressman fell for its star, Mercedes Rios.

Then the 'cast algorithm foisted this news segment on me about Nomura's stock plummeting. TFC let it slip that it had been negotiating with a Nomura rival, Mikota, to build mobiles compatible with TFC's application. *Rumor has it*, the business pundit commented, *that Nomura may be unable to deliver on Chipster deployment here and abroad.*

No wonder Dad is stressed. Good-bye billions.

I couldn't help being a tiny bit happy about that.

The mayor, standing in front of a TFC, then reiterated how important both Nomura and TFC were to the success of Hamilton's ID program and that he was sure they'd work out everything in time. The glint in his eyes said *or else*.

I turned down the volume, but left the commercial 'cast running, just in case the MemeCast broke in.

It didn't.

THE TWINKIE FACTORY

VELVET

The boys were skating at the old Twinkie factory on Salem Avenue. It was their go-to spot when they were bored. The place had been closed down for years, and no one had bought the joint for condos. The rumor was that the pipes were filled with Twinkie goo that had hardened—and were supporting the building structurally.

I pulled up a dusty crate and parked my jeans-clad butt to "watch." But, really, I was scribbling out some lyrics.

"Hey, where have you been?" Spike kicked his board in my direction, then plopped down on it beside me.

"Working. Stuff," I said, not looking up at him. I wasn't sure how to play this. Should I be honest? Should I just give it time? Aiden might disappear back to his preppy school this fall and I might never hear from him again. Was that fair to Spike? There were more important things going on.

"You okay? You don't seem your usual feisty self." He brushed away a hair from my forehead. "Missing Winter and Micah?" he guessed. "Me, too."

I shrugged. "Can I show you something?" I handed him my notebook, face open to a new song, "Chip in my Head." I thought it might be the best way to break it to them about the chip.

He took it gingerly and started reading. He glanced back at me a few times while he read.

"This is killer, Velvet," he finally said, full of serious-ness. Spike always took music (and art) seriously. "I had no idea." He leafed through a few more pages of poems and songs—lyrics only. I don't know how to read music. "Velvet Kowalcyk, you have unsuspected depths. Guys—"

"Wait—" I tried to stop him but he had already skated halfway across the warehouse floor—with my lyric book in hand.

Do not run. *Book of Velvet*.

By the time I strolled over, they were already working out the melody to the first song—well, playing air guitar to the first few stanzas.

"This stuff is Great, but we can't play it on the Bar Mitzvah/Quinceañera circuit," Richie said. "Too political. And dark." He was the money guy of the group.

"I want to play somewhere cool," Spike said. "I want to play something that matters."

"I just wanna get laid," Little Steven added, a bit forlornly.

"That better not be happening at the Bar Mitzvahs," Richie said.

Even I laughed at that. God, they were dim, but they were funny.

Spike looked at me. "What do you want, Velvet?"

"I want to do something." I pulled out Dune's wand from my backpack. "Steven, I saw your brother the other day."

Little Steven stopped laughing. I ran the wand behind his left ear. *Chime.*

Ditto with Spike and Richie.

"What the hell, Velvet?" Spike demanded.

So I told them. About the cop scanning me, about the ID chips implanted in our skulls, about the *Memento*s, about Winter and Micah, about Big Steven. About everything except for Aiden.

The testosterone flowed, and there was a lot of cursing and throwing of crates and skateboards.

When they'd calmed down, I said, "What if we played here in the factory? We could get the word out about what's going on." I tapped my head.

"You've been listening to the MemeCast too much." Richie groaned.

"Nah, it's perfect," Spike said as he drank in the space. "It'll be like our own underground rave."

I knew there was a reason I liked Spike.

"We'd better get busy then," I told him. It was only one week until D-day.

28.0

BETTER TO GIVE THAN TO DELETE

AIDEN

Another day, another zero dollars in cubicleland.

I stared at the function protocols for the model coming out in the fall.

No good.

I couldn't concentrate. The universe was muttering. I didn't want to think about Stepford Winter. The thought of her never being the same made me feel very unglossy. She was the only person that really knew me.

The terminal called my name. But where to start, I pondered as I held the testing headset in my hand.

The chip. I'd start with that. All my favorite people (both of them) seemed to have one. (And it kept coming up in the MemeCasts.)

I cracked my knuckles and applied my more-than-willing fingers to the keyboard. After poking around a little,

I found a back door into the project files that Roger or one of the other programmers had left.

Skid, huh?

Code jockeys, especially those with egos, always leave themselves a simple way to get back into a program or files, one they think only they will ever find. You just have to look for hints and pull on every door until one opens.

All the new mobiles—the Chipster, the Soma, etc.— were designed to work with this chip, the nGram, which could send and store data. The phone used frequencies— ones that decades ago were used for other purposes, like radio—to relay info to and from this chip. That's why the mobiles could pick up the MemeCast. But what use did that have? Sure, you could listen to tunes without earbuds and cheat on exams, but somehow that didn't seem like a wise investment of so much research and capital. If that was all the chip did.

Of course, there was the TFC app. *Forget your cares right from your home.* Did the app erase memories? That would be huge—and Not A Good Thing. At a TFC, you had to take a little white pill to forget. Could the company have truly figured out how to erase memories without the pill?

The universe started muttering again.

I opened another door. And there it was. Or, I should say, there *she* was. Dr. Hannah Ebbinghaus. Winter's doctor. While at the University of Hamilton, she developed the prototype of the nGram, which was originally designed to supply memories to Alzheimer's patients. I pulled up her research again. I didn't get the biology or the math, but the chip could be preprogrammed with information a senile patient might forget: his name, address, spouse, children, etc. The first version of the chip reinforced this information verbally over time. Patients retained more information than did the control group, who didn't have the chip.

It was the old Forgetting Curve thing; we'd learned about it in study skills class. (Bern Academy did not like you to flunk. *Anything*.) Memories fade over time—unless you periodically reinforce them. Translation: study every night. Right.

Version 2.0 of the nGram was supposed to reinforce memories chemically, through neurotransmitters. Nothing about whether this version was ever produced. But that's about the time Dr. Ebbinghaus joined Nomura.

Why would the company want a chip that reinforced memories? Language instruction? Learn German instantly? Memorize Shakespeare overnight?

Or could the TFC app add new memories as well as delete them? Maybe even things that never actually happened . . . ? Shudder. That would be A Very Bad Thing.

Someone coughed behind me. Roger.

I made no attempt to cover up the screen. Act innocent. Act like you have every right to be doing whatever they caught you doing.

Roger peered over my shoulder. "What the hell are you up to?"

"Just researching the products." When caught red-handed, tell the truth. Part of it at least. "It's about time I took an interest in the company."

To say Roger looked suspicious would be an under-statement.

I spun around slowly and looked him in the eye. "I will be running it someday." It was dirty, and I hated doing it.

"You've had everything handed to you." He leaned in. "You've never had to hack, crack, or scam—let alone break a sweat—a single day of your privileged life to feed yourself or your family. You aren't even a skid. You're a suit-in-training." He practically hissed the words.

I knew I'd asked for it, but it felt like he'd sucker-punched me. I'd never been flamed to my face before.

The universe wisely said nothing.

29.0
IT LIES

VELVET

I avoided the whole garage rehearsal scene as the boys worked out the music. I had some organizing to do.

The guys and gals at the Rocket Garden agreed to print up some flyers on their homemade press—which Dune said came from Winter's specs. I found out that his name is really An Dung Nyugen. I'd go by Dune, too.

"My brother's given name is even worse in English." Dune laughed. "He changed it to an Anglo one as soon as he could."

I was busy writing out the flyer in marker. I collaged together some generic band photos from an old magazine. The headline said MemeFest, and underneath it I printed "Free country, free concert" and June 30. I hesitated to put more.

It would be a bad idea to advertise the place and time

of an after-curfew, *Memento*-inspired concert that was happening hours before it became a crime not to have an ID chip.

But how would people know where it was? It was my first organizational snag.

Dune was rambling on about his brother's job and general geniusness. Their folks had run off to Saigon or Malaysia or someplace. I excused myself and went looking for Steven.

I found him and the short-haired woman inside the dome packing up boxes of radios. This time the chick was wearing a tank top and jeans, and I could see her tiger tattoo. Of course. Rebecca Starr. She'd been the Channel 5 reporter who'd gotten fired for making shit up. *Libel and incompetence*. How did I know that? It was like someone had whispered it to me.

"Don't believe the chip," Dune said from behind me. "It lies."

I spun around. "What?" I didn't need his scrawny ass in my head, too.

"That's what my brother says." Dune shrugged. "He used to help out here a lot."

Something wasn't quite right in brotherland.

"Roger is one of our graduates," Steven explained. "He works at Nomura." Steven tapped behind his ear.

Nomura made the ID chip.

"Do you mean—" I looked from Dune to Steven. Dune looked glum.

"Dune's worked out a security system for your concert," Steven said, changing the subject.

Dune brightened and launched into an explanation of his solar battery-charged lighting/alarm system.

"Whoa." I stopped him. "Too much information. You can run the system at the gig. And work the door."

"You bet," he said, and ran off muttering about finishing it in time.

Steven laughed. I could see he was trying to divert Dune's attention away from whatever was wrong between him and his brother. It was almost like Steven was trying to be Dune's big brother, or maybe trying to replace his own with Dune. Not cool.

"Little Steven could use some of that brothering," I told him.

Steven stiffened. "I know," he said finally. "But it hasn't been safe. Dad kicked me out when I went off-grid."

Damn. I was sorry I said it. It was a low blow, though I hadn't intended it to be. Little Steven missed his brother, and the whole situation just sucked. The silence was painfully awkward.

Rebecca helped us out. "You're a friend of Winter's, right? And the artist?" she asked. She lifted one of the sheets they'd been crumpling up as packing materials. It was a *Memento*.

I nodded. Rebecca Starr, I now remembered, was also the reporter who'd been in the video Aiden showed me, the one where Nora James gets arrested. Duh. That's why she got canned.

"Well, you should be careful with that," she said, indicating the flyer I still had in my hand. "Don't put the location on it."

"I was just thinking the same thing. But then how do I get the word out?"

"I can take care of that," Rebecca said. "I'll announce the time and place on the air."

Shit. She was the Meme Girl. She'd lost her job reporting on *Memento*, so she went off-grid to keep on reporting.

That took balls.

And a bakery truck. Becca—she said to call her Becca—asked Dune to take a look at something on her truck. I tagged along out of curiosity. The truck, which she'd parked as usual, outside the Rocket Garden gate, was a typical delivery van.

Inside, she pulled out a rack of muffins, and Dune ducked in front of her. He tinkered with something for a minute and declared it fixed. Then he helped himself to a blueberry muffin. Becca handed me one, too.

I wolfed it down and looked longingly at the rest. As usual, the cupboard was pretty bare at home. I wiped crumbs off my Rage Against the Machine T-shirt.

Becca pushed the rack back into place and shooed us out of the truck. She slid the door closed, and for the first time I noticed what it said: Black Dog Bakery.

The junkyard in my neighborhood, the one where Micah had lived, had a bakery. Mom had traded for stuff there all the time.

"Is this the same bakery . . ." I trailed off.

Becca nodded. "She set up shop—elsewhere. And the delivery truck is a good cover for my extracurricular activities." She smiled. "I can 'cast from anywhere."

Anywhere, huh? "How about the Twinkie Factory in five days?" I asked. If you don't ask, you don't get. *Book of Velvet*.

Becca hesitated. "Man, I really walked right into that one," she said with laugh. "Okay. But no one can know I'll be there 'casting until we go live. Even then I can't stay in one place too long."

"No problem," Dune said eagerly. "We can run a hardline from the band's sound system to the truck. You can just disconnect it and go whenever you need to."

"Cool," Becca said. She climbed into the driver's seat and closed the door after her.

"I can't wait to tell Roger." Dune grinned as he scamped back inside. He was even more excited about this than I was.

We are going to be on the MemeCast.

Spike was going to shit himself when I told him.

NEW DATA POINTS

AIDEN

Dad and I didn't say much at breakfast today. Cook made me coffee and something that approximated apple strudel. Dad just sipped his tea and read messages on his mobile. He grumbled about "breach of contract" but clammed up when I asked about it.

He flipped open his phone, told someone he'd "fight it" and he'd "tie them up in court for years," and then threw his mobile onto the table.

Dad flicked on the big screen at the other end of the room and put on a sports 'cast.

Dad hates sports.

And I didn't really want to talk to him, either.

This left me too many idle processing cycles to mull over things. I picked at the tough strudel crust. I'm much better at trusting my instincts (and the universe) than actual deductive reasoning. That was usually way too much work.

Okay. Focus. Sanity check. What are my data points?

One. There's a chip in Winter's (and Velvet's) heads that they don't remember getting.

Two. The chip only works with Nomura phones (for now, anyway).

Three. These phones are coming out early because of a TFC app—which must erase memory.

"Dad, how does the new TFC application work?" I asked reluctantly.

He looked away from the screen. "It's supposed to be like visiting a forgetting clinic," he said carefully. "You recount the memory into the app, and then the chip releases the neurochemical equivalent of the TFC drug to prevent the memory from resticking. The app also takes care of billing and reward points."

"But does it—" I was going to ask if it could plant memories as well. That might be data point four. The chip *could* reinforce memories. Theoretically.

He waved me off. "I don't understand the technical details."

Like hell he didn't. He knew exactly what was going on, and there was no use denying it to myself anymore. Dad was making a chip (and mobile) that could manipulate memories. With TFC.

I stabbed the strudel with my fork.

Dad took a renewed interest in some news item or message on his mobile.

I should confront him. But then what?

The strained silence between us was smashed by Uncle Brian and Aunt Spring rushing into the breakfast room. I immediately thought it must be about Winter.

Man, was I wrong.

"Ichiro, we're so sorry, but we didn't remember until this morning." My uncle looked like he actually wanted to kowtow to Dad.

"Aiden-kun, we know this must be a difficult time for you. And we feel terrible for not acknowledging it sooner." Spring cast a look in Brian's direction. "We're here to help with whatever preparations you've planned."

Dad and I shared a look of total blankness.

"What are you talking about?" I asked finally.

"It's been a year, Aiden-kun," my aunt said gently.

"A year?" I was feeling really stupid. I had no clue what she was talking about.

"I can't believe we almost forgot," Brian said, incredulous. "We couldn't be here then, but we're here now."

Dad rose, slipped on his jacket, and headed toward the door. "I do not have time for whatever this is," he called over his shoulder.

My aunt and uncle looked stunned.

"But, Ichiro, your wife died a year ago today," Brian said.

That stopped Dad in his proverbial tracks. I think I dropped my fork.

"You must have planned a memorial service," Spring added.

"What the hell are you talking about?" Dad demanded as he crossed the room.

"Gretchen. The car accident in the Alps," Brian said uncertainly.

Dad hit the speed dial on his mobile. Brian and Spring looked at me.

"Mom is not dead," I managed to say. "She picked me up at school and took me to the airport. I've talked to her four or five times since then."

Brian and Spring stared at me and then each other, like they weren't sure whether to check me or themselves into a mental ward. I glanced at Dad, who was still talking to someone. Mom, I presumed. He nodded at me and flipped his mobile shut.

"Your mother is in a meeting now, but she'll call you tonight," Dad told me with a profound (for him) look of relief on his face. Then he turned on his brother.

"What the fuck was that about, Brian?"

I saw Uncle Brian flinch, and I didn't have to see Dad's face to know what it looked like. I'd gotten that face many times. Although Brian was probably getting it tenfold.

"But we remember the . . ." Aunt Spring trailed off.

"Wait. Did you say you just remembered it this

morning?" I asked. "Both of you? At the same time?"

I did look at Dad now. His face was ashen.

Holy crap.

Dad's mobile buzzed, and he stood looking at the message for at least thirty seconds. Then he dashed out the door.

New data points. *Four. The chip does plant memories. Five. Ichiro Nomura is scared.*

31.0

THE UNIVERSE PIMP-SLAPS ME

AIDEN

Sometimes the universe slaps you across the face, and all of the pieces click into place—and the picture wasn't what you'd thought it was. At all. Brian and Spring in "Japan." Mom and I getting shipped off to Switzerland. Winter on meds.

Dad wasn't in bed with TFC to make money. He was there because he didn't have a choice. He sent Mom and me away to protect us.

Only he hadn't gotten to Uncle Brian and Aunt Spring in time. They'd been "disappeared" to Detention. And when Winter remembered the truth, Dad had his doctor dope her up.

Dad never wanted to be part of TFC's plans for this chip. Or for whatever else they had planned. He was trying to protect all of us.

I felt both profoundly relieved and scared shitless at the same time.

My mom being "dead"—that was a threat.

Aunt Spring and Uncle Brian stood there, blinking at me.

"Okay, what just happened?" Spring asked.

I didn't tell them.

I didn't know if I could help—or trust them. (Steven might have a point about people with chips in their heads.)

But it wasn't too late for Winter.

32.0

BRINGING WINTER BACK

AIDEN

I told Jao to take my aunt and uncle back home, and then I took a cab to see Mr. Yamada. I had to be sure of something first. On the way, I checked a few records. Then I stopped by the drugstore and bought a bottle of vitamins. D, I think.

• • •

Mr. Yamada answered the door in his track pants and a sweaty T-shirt. Winter had told me all about the obstacle course he'd built to work out on. He led me into the kitchen and motioned for me to sit at the counter.

"Can I get you something to drink?" he asked as he peeled off his half-fingered gloves and tossed them on the counter. I'd seen rock climbers wear those kind of gloves. They protect your hands while letting you grip ledges and handholds. That must be some interesting course.

"Coffee, if you have it."

He pushed a cup and a plate of cookies in my direction. "Is Winter okay?" he asked.

"No." It hurt me as much to say it as it did to watch his reaction.

He sank onto the other stool, and I told him about my last visit to her house.

"We went through this when I took her to a doctor years ago. We tried the meds for a while, but Winter said she couldn't think straight. And I agreed to let her stop taking them. I guess I shouldn't have, but it was so hard to watch her foggy and listless."

"What did the doctor say she had back then?"

"Bipolar disorder—more manic than depressive. He said it was very manageable, though. The art helps her focus her energy."

"This new doc is treating her for paranoid schizophrenia, but I don't think there's anything wrong with Winter. Except that she's overmedicated."

"What makes you say that?" His eyes narrowed. At least he didn't call me crazy.

"Winter was right. Spring and Brian weren't in Japan."

Mr. Yamada got to his feet. "They were in Japan working for the company, but they're home now. Everything is finally okay. Winter can get on with her life. Forget about art. Work hard. Go to school. A good school. Work for the company."

Déjà vu.

I thought about asking him if my mom was alive, but he saved me the trouble.

"I have no idea why I said that." He shook his head and sank back onto the stool. "It's like some little voice is whispering it in my head, but deep down I know it's not true."

"Do you feel like you've been brain-bleached?"

He'd been told he was in the hospital with a concussion. Another lie.

Mr. Yamada nodded. "My friends say I was but they're afraid to tell me more. Trying to protect me, I guess. And this is going to sound weird, but especially after I work out or get into the groove tattooing, I feel like some of my memories aren't really mine. They're hazy ghosts of memories."

"Really? Like what?"

"Like the mugging. The whole Japan thing. I remember the intense emotions—the anger, the stress, the fear. I felt like something had happened to Spring. I wake up at night dreaming about finding Winter alone in her house, hiding in the dryer. That doesn't match this hazy memory I have of dropping Spring off at the airport. It's like someone told me about it." He rubbed behind his ear absently.

"When did you get that ID chip?" I asked. From what Winter had said, Mr. Yamada wasn't the type to have one.

He turned pale as he carefully felt the outline of the chip under his skin. "Is that what it is? The doctor told

me someone cracked me on the head when I was patrol-
ling the neighborhood. Damn. I'd never get an ID chip.
Especially in my head." He paused. "Winter has one, too,
doesn't she?"

I nodded. He swore softly in Japanese.

"Ready to get our Winter back?" I shook the bottle of
vitamins I'd bought earlier.

"What are they?" he asked.

"Vitamins," I said. I pulled out the pill I'd taken from
Winter's medicine cabinet. "They just happen to look
exactly like meds for a so-called paranoid schizophrenic."

33.0

SCENE FROM A SHOPPING MALL

VELVET

We'd gotten pretty ballsy about handing out the Meme-Fest flyers. Since school was out, I hit the lesser shopping centers—the ones without much security—and left the flyers in the bathroom stalls. (Becca said that had a certain symmetry since that's how *Memento* started.) The flyers didn't have the place or time on them. You had to listen to the MemeCast to get the concert dates. We now had several planned, with the first being on June 30—the eve of D-day for the new ID chips. D-day for those going off-grid.

Even though D-day was only a few days away, Mom was still deciding about the chip. Or still putting off deciding, which amounted to the same thing. Tick tock.

The guys and I were hanging out in the food court of the Valley Ridge Mall. A short bus ride from downtown, the place is a run-down shopping center that doesn't even require an ID to get in the door.

Richie and Little Steven were talking about which actress they'd have an affair with: Mercedes Rios of *Behind the Gates* or Carmen Washington of that new 'cast, *Under the Dome*.

Spikey was intent on replacing his back skateboard wheels with a new set he'd just traded for.

I stole a greasy chili fry off his plate as I watched people filter by. They were mostly kids like us. No money, no chips (that they officially knew of), and no place else to hang out in the growing heat. A few older women in sneakers power-walked laps around the mall. A guy dozed upright on the bench across from the DQ. His head bobbed and he caught himself every few minutes. The minute he lay down security would toss him out. Even in this mall, they didn't like homeless people camping out during the day.

Then I saw her and her BFFs sit down, bags in hand, by the fountain.

It was Nora James.

She was eating a cookie and laughing with her friends, Maia Jackson and Abby Delgado—like nothing had ever happened to her. They were admiring a pair of red shoes, and I heard "Quinceañera" and "party" rise above the din. Abby must be having her Quince this summer.

How was this possible? Duh. I knew how. Nora's memory got whitewashed, and they let her go on her merry popular-girl way.

Still. I wondered if she'd come to the concert. If some of that old Nora James was lurking in there.

The BFFs made like they were leaving.

Now or never.

I peeled my ass off the hard plastic chair and moved toward them. Spike caught my hand.

"Careful," he whispered, glancing up at the security cams.

I leaned over to kiss him on the forehead, and he placed a folded up flyer into the palm of my hand. This time I kissed him on the lips. He tasted like chili fries.

Spike was a little rough around the edges, but you knew where you stood with him. Aiden was smooth, too smooth, but when you peeled back his glossy exterior, he was intriguing, unpredictable, and intense.

This was not a problem I'd expected to have. Ever.

But I'd deal with it later.

I had something more important to do just then.

SCENE PART TWO

VELVET

Nora, Maia, and Abby were already heading toward the street exit, but I could hear their convo as I half jogged up from behind, breaking my own rule about running.

"If you don't want to stay with your mom, I'm sure mine will let you sleep over," Maia said as she put her arm around Nora.

"Or you can stay with me." Abby moved to flank Nora.

"Thanks, but we need to work out this divorce thing." Nora wriggled free from Maia's grasp. "And I'm not so sure she's making things up anymore."

"You can't be serious," Maia said, disbelief in her voice.

"Hold up," I called as they headed outside.

Nora stopped, though Maia was urging her not-too-gently toward a waiting car. I could see Mrs. Jackson behind the wheel—she waved at me.

"Maia!" I called her name and stood my ground. Make them come to you. *Book of Velvet*.

She stopped pushing Nora and faced me. Maia Jackson was an All-State JV tennis champ and had the arms to prove it. Nora was doing pretty well holding her own against those biceps.

"Velvet." Maia looked me up and down.

I ignored her and turned to Nora. "There's a concert at the Twinkie Factory." I pressed the folded-up flyer into her hand. I held on to it when she tried to pull away. "Micah will be there," I whispered. "And so will the MemeCast."

Nora's eyes dilated. Did she remember?

I let her hand drop and spun on my heel. I didn't look back once, though I heard Abby call me a freak. Maia hushed her.

I kept on walking.

As I strode inside, I envisioned a shell-shocked Nora being hustled off into the waiting car.

Spike said that's exactly what happened.

NO PLACE IS SAFE NOW

AIDEN

As I stepped on the Skywalk, I heard a rumble in the distance like thunder. I shrugged it off. My mind was on Winter.

I'd switched the pills, which was far easier than I'd thought. Winter slept through most of my visit—and the maid was glued to her earbuds listening to a 'cast as she halfheartedly dusted.

I stopped at Starbucks and then walked toward the Nomura offices. The caramel macchiato made me feel only marginally better.

Hopefully, the fog would clear from Winter's brain, and her implant would stop working—again—because of her different brain chemistry. But what aboutpeople with so-called normal brains? Her parents? Mr. Yamada? Anyone else who had one of these chips? Or bought one of our phones? I couldn't make other people's brain chemstry like Winter's.

But I could erase the chip. Maybe. If it wasn't encrypted. That's what I had to figure out, and Nomura was the easiest place to do it. And I could check on Dad, too.

Someone rushed past me, nearly spilling my coffee.

That's when I saw the burning remains of a car parked in the visitor lot outside Nomura headquarters. Tamarind Bay security had blocked off the front entrance while firefighters doused the flames. I'd never heard of a bombing inside of a compound. That was the whole point of living in one.

I stared at the charred remains of the vehicle.

"No place is safe now," an onlooker said to me.

I made for the side entrance.

• • •

I was relieved to see Dad there as I crept by his office. He was talking to some non-Nomura suit. Was it the mayor? Jao stood outside the door next to a slick-looking guy in shades with a Green Zone tag and a Vote Mignon button on his dark jacket.

Roger was on the phone when I walked into the lab, arguing with someone in Vietnamese. I nodded at him before sitting down at the screen. I pulled up the Chipster schematics. I could transmit an old-fashioned virus to overwrite the data.

The Russian boards were good for that kind of shit. Okay, I was a skid. But a virus might wipe out the ID information stored on the chip, too, which I didn't want. Maybe there was some simple command I could send that would shut down the feed. Or maybe I could override the content with something new. The thought made me shudder.

I tried to pull up the implant specs but got shut out.

Access denied.

Of course, my father picked that moment to walk into the lab. *Funny timing*, the universe muttered. I watched Dad cross the room. I knew what was coming.

· · ·

"Aiden, why are you here?" Dad asked in a hoarse whisper. He paused to glance over his shoulder. The Green Zone goon stood by the door, along with Jao.

"Dad, I know what's going on. I can help," I whispered back.

He closed his eyes for a second and then looked me in the eye. "Stay out of it, Aiden. You're in way over your head. And so am I," he added quietly.

"You're fired," Dad said loudly. He slipped something into my backpack. "If anything happens to me, Jao will get you to your mother," he whispered. "Take this with you." He shoved my pack into my hands. "Jao will drive you home."

Jao dutifully stepped up behind my father.

"Don't lose him this time," Dad told Jao. Then he stormed out of the room, the Green Zone guy hot on his heels. Jao stared after Dad and the goon. Yeah, not good.

And Roger was nowhere in sight.

Jao dragged me home.

36.0

EXTRA-CURRICULAR ACTIVITY

AIDEN

Jao paced the foyer. Extra security patrolled outside.

Me, I sat at the kitchen table, staring at the contents of my backpack, while the big screen blared the news.

Dad had slipped a small black package into my bag. Turning it over in my hands, I still didn't know what to do. I could just leave it and let Dad keep protecting us. But what if he never came home?

I called Mom. Again. No answer.

News gal reported that two dozen cities were announcing mandatory ID programs. She cut to a news conference at TFC headquarters. Some suit said Cleveland, Atlanta, Detroit, and Pittsburgh would be requiring its citizens to get the nGram ID chip by Christmas. The other cities would stagger their deadlines over the next year. All were implementing their programs with the generous help of TFC. The camera pulled back to reveal the TFC logo on the wall behind her. The camera panned to show more suits off to the side. Dad was there, sandwiched between the mayor and the Green Zone guy. Dad rubbed behind his ear as the camera passed him.

I had to do something.

So I opened the package. The grin on my face made Jao stop pacing. Inside the little box were a chip and microdisk, which I promptly popped into my mobile.

nGram chip schematics scrolled across my screen.

Dad had given me the exact thing I'd been trying to access in the office.

He'd promised me interesting doors to rattle.

And the disk contents told me two things. One. The datastream was encrypted. That is, it took one, possibly two keys to unlock this door. Normally, I could charm those keys out of someone, just like I'd done with the bank encryption.

Except for data point two. TFC owned the code. They (and their security minions) are notoriously hard to charm.

Someone at Nomura might have access to the encryption. They'd need it to test the chip. Maybe. One person would know.

Roger.

Unfortunately, Jao wasn't letting me out of his sight until Dad got home.

I fell asleep turning over glossy hard bits of code in my mind looking for a door handle to pull.

. . .

When Jao shook me awake, I was slumped over the kitchen table. "Master Aiden, your father's home—and he has *company*." He said the last part with distaste as he pushed the chip and my mobile toward me. I stuffed them in my pocket.

Dad walked in the front door followed by the Green Zone guy from the office.

"You can wait outside," Dad told him.

The guy hesitated, and Jao moved toward him, bristling.

"I'm not going anywhere," Dad snapped at the goon, "except maybe to bed." He looked exhausted.

The goon took up position inside the front door. Dad let it go.

"Are you okay?" I asked him. I was afraid of what he wouldn't remember.

Dad nodded, but he also tapped behind his right ear. He looked from me to the contents of the backpack, still spread on the kitchen table, then back to me.

"Aiden, don't you have some extracurricular activity today?" Dad asked. My mind was a blank. "Some doors to rattle on maybe," he whispered.

I nodded.

"Jao will drive you wherever you need to go," Dad said as he headed toward his bedroom.

The goon at the door just stared straight ahead.

RETURN OF THE HUMMINGBIRDS

WINTER

When I woke up this morning, my head felt clear. That full of pudding feeling was gone. I hate pudding. Now, my skull felt empty, blissfully hollow. I vaguely remembered Aiden stopping by yesterday. Or was it days ago? Hard to tell. It was right before Mom pressed another damn pill in my hand. He'd banged around in my bathroom as I dozed off.

Mom had given me another pill after lunch, too, but I spit it out.

The hummingbirds were back.

I held out my hand in front me. No tremor. Not a twitch.

Thoughts began to tumble freely through my brain, no longer weighted down by the pills.

The pills.

My parents and that doctor had drugged me. Because

they thought I was sick. Because . . . A hummingbird slammed into a residual chunk of pudding, and I couldn't complete the thought.

I needed to do something. I pulled myself out of the lounge chair. I needed to tinker. I needed to get out of here.

I walked out the door, down the block, and took the Skywalk to the edge of Tamarind Bay. I caught the bus downtown.

12:35 PM. SOMEWHERE IN THE CITY OF HAMILTON . . .

Decision time, citizens. Tick tock. D-day approaches.

And the little demonstration over at Tamarind Bay was just a small reminder that compound gates and security guards aren't enough to keep you safe anymore.

You know what you need, and you're running out of time to get it—before Mayor Mignon's promised crackdown commences.

So, do you continue being a good citizen? Do you get yourself chipped and keep keeping on, fully gridded? Or do you slip through the cracks in the grid and join us below its radar?

You may be saying, "Whoa, Meme Girl or whatever you call yourself, unwrap the tinfoil from your pointy head. It's just a chip."

Maybe.

Maybe not.

Let me tell you a story about a friend of a friend. It's a short story. One day he's a cop, bumped down to searching book bags at a high school for something he saw and reported. So he watches for black vans at night on his own time. Then he finds a group of like-minded individuals, falls in love, helps a girl—and wham. He's shipping out to fight in the oil fields for a four-year tour like it's his own idea. That's another one of those stories you don't hear.

Next: "Going Underground" by the Jam.

38.0

BACK TO THE ROCKET GARDEN

VELVET

Do not volunteer for something until you're sure it doesn't include manual labor. *Book of Velvet.*

Maybe I need a new book, I told myself as I wrestled shrink wrap around a pallet of boxes in the courtyard of the Rocket Garden. Each of them was marked CANNED FOOD, but that's not what they contained. Who knew the local food pantry dished out a little revolution on the side?

I wiped the sweat from my face with the tail of my Ramones T-shirt and climbed back up to the dome. Inside Becca, Lanky Girl (a.k.a., Lina), Big Steven, and I were packing up the radios we'd made. It was almost July, and it would've been as sweltering inside the dome as out, if Lina hadn't rigged up a tiny air conditioner. She was clever, but not much of a conversationalist.

"Is Dune coming in today?" I asked. He at least liked to talk.

"Haven't seen him." Steven shrugged. "The food bank guy will be here after dark to pick up the radios," he said, changing the subject. "We need to hustle to pack this last stack of boxes and lift the pallets over the fence." Steven had built this small crane out of spare radio tower parts to lug things around the Garden.

"Yessir," I said, diving back into the radio packing. When Steven had a bug up his butt about getting something done, it was best not to mess with him.

I wrapped a plain plastic box with hand-painted dials in old paper and stuffed it into a cardboard box. Winter would have made these things look cool with gears and copper tubes and stuff. Hell, I'd never even seen a radio before meeting this crew. The radios were like something out of a history book on consumer electronics, but Becca said they could pick up the MemeCast and anything else on those frequencies. And if they picked up the MemeCast, they'd pick up the concert. It was going to be epic.

"Incoming!" one of the guys yelled from the courtyard.

"Hide the radios," Steve said quietly as he strode toward the door. His bulk filled the door frame, blotting out a bit of the daylight.

"Where?" I looked around quickly. We were in the middle of a hollowed-out piece of machinery with only a bunch of folding tables and chairs.

"In the boxes." Lina was already stuffing the empty boxes with radios, and I followed suit.

"False alarm." Steven stepped aside, and I heard footsteps coming up the ladder. "It's your boyfriend. The new one."

Lina glared at me and at all the boxes we now had to empty and repack.

"Actually, I need to talk to Dune," Aiden said to Steven without even looking in my direction. There was something manic in his voice. It reminded me of Winter. Winter on one of her not-so-good days.

"Aiden, what's the matter?" I was by his side before I even realized it. He shrugged off my touch.

"Sorry, I don't have time to explain, but I need to find Roger." He looked from me to Steven. I wasn't sure who he was apologizing to or asking.

"Don't you work with him?" I asked.

"He's gone, and I got kicked out. Dad's in trouble. I need Roger's help," Aiden said without taking a breath.

Steven disappeared.

"Slow down. What's going on?" I'd never seen Aiden upset.

"I'll explain later."

Steven reappeared and handed Aiden a small padded envelope. "Roger left this for you. Take it and go. We've got work to do here."

That last part was directed at me. I took the hint

and guided Aiden toward the door. My heart ached to see him like this. Scared. "What can I do?" I asked.

His mobile buzzed as we hit daylight.

"Slow down," he said into the phone as he clambered down the steps. He stopped and listened.

"I'll be right back," I called to Steven as I followed Aiden to the courtyard.

"Don't worry, Aunt Spring. I'll find her." Aiden snapped his mobile shut. "It's Winter. She's missing."

Instead of panic, though, I saw relief on Aiden's face.

"It worked." He grinned.

I didn't have a clue what he was talking about.

"Don't worry. I know exactly where she is." He pecked me on the cheek and took off running.

"Bring her to the concert!" I yelled after him.

I immediately regretted it. When you don't know what to say, do not scream something self-centered and lame. *Book of Velvet*. New chapter. New verse.

39.0
BACK TO THE GARDEN

WINTER

I slipped in the back way, through the semi-secret panel in the fence. I wasn't quite ready to talk to Grandfather yet. The hummingbirds were still battling the pudding in my brain. *Damn pills. I'll never take another one again. Not even an aspirin.*

Grandfather's *Sasuke* course looked like someone had begun stripping the parts and dismantling it. *Maybe he's redoing it,* I told myself. He wouldn't give up on it. He'd used the course every day since I'd moved in.

I pushed through the bamboo gate, through the garden, and into my workshop. I grabbed some circuit boards, a soldering iron, and a sheet of milky white Plexiglas.

I had this vision in my head of a wall of bird wings that reacted to your movement, curling and flittering as you got closer, rippling as you walked along the wall. I scrounged through my buckets of circuit boards and found a motion activator. I cut out a test sliver of the Plexiglas in a wing shape.

The hummingbird wings in my head calmed to a dull flutter as I started soldering chips and dipswitches and connectors.

I'd missed this. I needed this. I was this. And I could make this installation huge.

"Winter?"

Crap.

At least it wasn't Mom or Dad. It was Aiden. I turned around to find him and Grandfather both looking at me as if they expected me to say something momentous. It was unnerving—and really bugged the shit out of me.

"What?" I didn't mask my annoyance very well. "Can't you see I'm working?"

"Yes!" Aiden did a little fist pump thing like he'd scored a goal. "She's back."

Grandfather just smiled and said *he'd* be right back.

"You have been a zombie—Stepford Winter—for the past few weeks." Aiden wrapped me in a hug.

"Stupid pills," I muttered.

"That's why I substituted vitamin D for them." The shiny things on the workbench caught his attention. He picked up my prototype. "What are you making?"

"You switched my pills?" Why didn't I think of that? Because my brain was full of pudding, and I thought my parents had my best interests at heart. It made me happier than I could describe to know my cousin had my back like that. "Thanks," I said quietly. I was trying really hard not to cry.

"You needed the vitamins. You don't get enough sun—usually." He was trying not to look at me.

"Oh, shut up." I took the circuit board from his hand.

It was good to be back. Grandfather brought out two mugs of double-espresso, six-sugar love.

Okay, Aiden's had only four sugars.

Aiden's happy mask slipped away as he sipped his coffee.

"It's your dad, isn't it?" I asked.

"You were right about Japan," Aiden replied.

"I'd started to put it together before the doctor drugged me."

Aiden explained everything he'd figured out about the chip, his Dad's involvement, right up to the freakish demonstration with my parents.

"*Kuso*," Grandfather swore.

"Then there was the bombing in the Nomura parking lot—and the mayor and some Green Zone goons paid a visit to Dad at the office—right before he sent me home with Jao."

Aiden paused.

"Dad came home this morning—with a chip in his head and a new bodyguard," Aiden continued quietly.

Holy crap.

"We have to stop them," he said.

I had more questions, many more, but they could wait. We had to get our family back—all of them.

Grandfather and I nodded.

"Before they do whatever they're gonna do July first," Aiden added.

That didn't give us much time. About forty-eight hours.

40.0
TICK TOCK

AIDEN

We retreated to Winter's workshop. Mr. Yamada said he had some appointments at his shop—but not to do anything stupid yet. At least not until he got back.

"So we need to hack TFC. Without them knowing. And then stop them. All in two days?" Winter asked.

"Not exactly," I replied. "Well, I hope not. We just need to send a signal to the chip to erase the embedded memories or shut down the feed."

"Is that all?" Winter laughed. "It might be easier if we had a chip."

"Good thing I have one." I dumped my backpack on the table. The package Dad had given me and Roger's mystery envelope lay there among the other detritus of my life. "Dad gave me this," I said, handing Winter the package. Then I opened the envelope from Roger. Inside was a black plastic square about 3.5 inches in size. It was a museum piece. "Are you kidding me?"

"Roger must have given you that," she said casually.

"How did you know?" I waggled the disk at Winter.

She took it from me and popped it into an ancient computer under her workbench.

"Do you know what workshop he taught at the Rocket Garden?"

She didn't wait for me to answer.

"How to build your own underground network out of scrap and outdated tech. Like this." She uncovered an old flatscreen monitor. "And that," she added, pointing to a series of routers atop one of the shelves.

A real underground network. A network like this had the range of a few hundred square feet. Doesn't sound like much—until you tie a bunch of these handmade networks together.

"Is that what you're running your garden on?" I asked. Each moving statue seemed to interact with the next and could be controlled remotely.

Winter nodded. "In exchange, I showed Roger how to make an FM transmitter."

And your transmitter broadcasts on the same frequency as the chip and the MemeCast. This was no coincidence. Was Roger the technical wizard behind the MemeCast—and did he have plans for it all along?

"So what's on the disk?" I asked.

"Hell if I know." She spun the monitor toward me.

The disk was encrypted.

"Typical Roger paranoia," Winter muttered.

"Not so paranoid if people are after you."

The code scrawled across the old monitor. It was very hard to visualize it in 2-D, but it looked a little familiar. I clunked around on the old fashioned keyboard for a while but couldn't seem to turn the code over in my mind. I pulled out my mobile, disconnected it from the grid, and downloaded the code.

And there it was. A hard, glossy knot of gorgeous code with no visible door to pull on.

This was the encryption Mom had given me to crack on the plane. The new encryption algorithm of Banc Raush. Or was it? Did TFC pressure her company, too? Had they developed the code for memories rather than money? Data was data.

I still had the decryption key on my mobile.

The door unlocked.

> If you can read this, you're no skid—and you have the key to decoding the implanted memory stream on the nGram. It took me a month of brute force attack to crack the other key, the one to encode the data (and this message). Unfortunately I couldn't work out the decryption key in time.
>
> Forgive me, but I had to protect my family. I hope you get this before the 1st and can figure out what to do with the keys.

A long line of numbers and letters wrapped across the bottom of the screen. The other key.

With both, I could hack the ID chips.

But we just needed one more thing.

TFC communicated with the chip on the same frequency as Winter's FM transmitter—and the MemeCast.

"We need to call Velvet," I said finally.

41.0

REVENGE OF THE CLOWN CAKE

VELVET

Big night.

Everything was set. Aiden and Winter's plan was a no-brainer for me. Becca agreed, too. Now I could really do something. *I hope they make it to the concert.*

I set up Lina at the door with a walkie, a police scanner, and the panic button Steven's crew had made. Dune was still a no-show. Lina explained the security system. The battery-run lights would flash if the cops were on their way. I told her to hit it if she saw anything suspicious, too. Oh, and no alcohol through the door. We didn't want people getting stupid.

The band began their sound check. Now I just had to wait and see if anyone showed.

My biggest fear is throwing a party and no one shows up.

It happened to me in sixth grade. I'd invited a handful of popular girls—like Maia Jackson, who I'd been friends with in elementary school—to my birthday party. No one showed up—or even asked about the party later. It was just me and Mom and my grandmother and a huge clown-shaped ice cream cake she'd picked out.

I haven't thrown a party since.

A former chapter in the *Book of Velvet*.

The band finished its sound check. I was having clown-cake flashbacks as I watched the door. Nada.

Aiden probably wasn't coming, either.

Why did I say no alcohol?

Spike jumped down from the stage, which wasn't much more than a bunch of wooden pallets nailed together. He slung his arm around my shoulders. "They'll come. Curfew be damned."

I had to admit that Spike knew when to say the right thing. I kissed his cheek. He took my face gently in his hand and planted a wet one on my lips. After a second, I returned the kiss gratefully.

"Get a room, you two," a voice said from the door. Big Steven and his crew strolled in—followed by a stream of kids.

"They got lost." Steven jerked his thumb toward the crowd beginning to fill up the entry.

I told Spike to go get ready.

"Oh, I'm ready," he said adjusting his crotch.

I had to admit that Spike also knew how to say the

wrong thing at the right time. He grinned and leaned in to give me another quick kiss.

I shook my head and pushed him toward the stage. He was still grinning.

I started shooing the partiers toward the stage and refreshment area (sodas only). While I was doing that, I heard the Steven reunion playing out behind me.

"Little bro, you've grown." Little brother was now taller than big brother. Big Steven wrapped Little Steven in a bear hug. Micah always said their parents had no imagination.

Micah. I scanned the growing sea of faces for him. He should be out of juvie by now, and I hoped he'd seen one of the flyers.

The band was about to take the stage when I spotted his curly mop trying to push its way through the crowd. I waded in but didn't make much headway.

"Micah!" I called. The crowd let him through.

The guys saw him, too. They jumped off the platform and practically tackled him before I even had a chance to say a word.

Things were working out far better than I'd expected. If only Winter and Aiden would get here, then we'd all be together again.

Micah explained that he'd just gotten out of juvie last week. He'd tried to call everyone, but his mobile was blocked. He'd gotten our flyer from someone at the food bank, where he was doing his community service.

We spelled out everything the best we could—about the *Memento*s and how he'd been brain-bleached—but he hardly believed what had happened. (Micah was our resident conspiracy theory nut, but I guess you don't believe it when it's really happening to you.)

The crowd started chanting "play, play."

I motioned the guys toward the stage. We'd have plenty of time to catch up later.

The crowd stopped chanting as Spike strapped on his guitar and walked to the mike. He tapped it a few times and cleared his throat.

"Before we get started," he said, "let's give a shout out to my girl, Velvet, for organizing this whole thing."

The crowd chanted "Velvet" until Spike pulled me up on stage.

I was floating.

42.0

A LITTLE DINNER MUSIC

WINTER

The front door announced that we had visitors.

They came. What a relief. Part one of our plan was coming together.

I answered the door, just in case they were still pissed at Grandfather.

"Honey, we were so worried about you." Mom went all motherly on me, hugging me and checking out my new-old attire with a shake of her head. I had dyed the tips of my hair purple. Mom was trying to make the best of it.

Dad hugged me and told me to never, ever run away again.

Uncle Ichiro brought up the rear. He nodded at me and told his new Green Zone bodyguard to wait outside.

"It's a family dinner," Uncle Ichiro said impatiently when the goon hesitated. The guard planted himself outside the front door.

I brought everyone out to the dining table we'd set up in the garden. Mom glared at her own father as he offered her a drink. Dad whispered something to her.

Aiden hugged his father like they hadn't seen each other in three years.

Time for some music. I pressed a button on the remote, and the solar chimes started to play a soft acoustic guitar instrumental thing. I figured that was neutral enough for dinner dining—and deprogramming.

"Mom, I want you and Grandfather to bury the hatchet. And not in each other's foreheads," I told her as I showed her to her seat.

That made Dad laugh uneasily.

When I'd called them earlier, I had let them believe this whole thing was about reconciliation. It was. Sort of.

Aiden and I helped Grandfather serve dinner. (He'd actually ordered it from this Cuban place a few blocks away. We aren't good cooks.)

We all made uncomfortable chitchat over roast pork and black beans. I nibbled on some *tostones* while I watched Mom and Dad for a sign, any sign. Aiden, I noticed, wouldn't look at Uncle Ichiro and vice versa. They both pushed the pork and onions around their plates in little circles.

Time for the reconciliation part of the evening. We were about to find out if my parents' fake memories had successfully been wiped.

"Mom and Dad, I'm sorry I left without telling you. But please stop punishing Grandfather for whatever you think he did." I winked at Grandfather as I said this. He busied himself with another piece of pork.

"He let you—" Mom stopped.

"What? Go crazy? No. He took really great care of me while you were gone. He let me be myself. And if you don't like who I am, then that's your problem."

"But you were saying some craz—mixed-up things," my dad said.

"What? That I didn't think you were in Japan? Search your memory, both of you. Right now. Do you really remember being there? Humor me. Oh, and by the way, Aunt Gretchen? Not dead."

Aiden was staring at his father. Uncle Ichiro kept his eyes on his plate.

My father thought about it for a second or two and turned to Mom. "Honey?"

"Oh, come on. Where else would we have been?" She looked at Ichiro for support. He studied his empanada.

"Dad, we figured it out. The chip. The encryption. Everything," Aiden said.

Here's where I expected Uncle Ichiro to fly into a rage. He simply looked up at Aiden and smiled. "I knew you would," he said.

My parents just stared.

"Really?" Aiden asked.

"Really," Uncle Ichiro said.

I wanted to cry, and I hate crying.

"Did they do anything to you? Besides the chip?" Aiden asked quietly.

My uncle shook his head. "They said it was better I remember exactly what I have to lose."

A tear slid down Aiden's cheek, and his father wrapped his arm around Aiden.

So we'd gotten our families back, even though mine was still befuddled by the whole thing.

"Would someone please explain what's going on?" my mother asked.

"Later, Mom. I promise," I said. My teary, huggy urges had passed. "We have a concert to get to," I told Aiden.

He nodded and wiped his face on his sleeve.

43.0

BONFIRE OF THE WANNABES

VELVET

The Wannabes started playing "Anything Girl," one of my songs. I couldn't help thinking I'd finally accomplished something, even if it was just an abandoned warehouse with a bunch of friends playing my half-assed song. But all these people were here. And so was the MemeCast. Becca was broadcasting it to her van, and from there to all the other mobiles and radios and whatevers out there in Hamilton.

Micah made a drinking motion and mouthed that he'd be right back. I pointed in the direction of the table along the back wall. I hoped he was okay with soda.

The crowd clapped, hooted even, for the first song and the next one. I was still floating. I looked around, hoping to see Aiden and Winter. Big Steven gave me the thumbs up.

I caught sight of Micah, and he seemed to be doing his own floating. The crowd in front of him had parted, revealing none other than—you guessed it—Nora James.

Why did I invite her? Well, she did sort of start all this.

She was backing away slowly. Finally she stopped, and they stood there gawking at each other, still standing fairly far apart. It wasn't like one of those movie rush-into-each-other's-arms kind of things. It was more of an excuse-me-do-I-know-you-and-are-you-stalking-me thing on her part. But the crowd knew the story and seemed to be pushing them together. And Micah and Nora were beginning to feel their strange attraction. They inched forward as they shouted over the band.

Maia Jackson was tugging Nora's elbow, trying to pull her toward the door. I moved to Micah's side, nodding at Maia as I took up position.

"We have got to get out of here," Maia yelled at Nora.

Nora was transfixed. "Micah?" She looked like someone who thinks they know you but can't quite place your face.

Then Tom Slayton burst through the door. Lina looked at me to see if she should hit the panic button. I held up my hand. *Wait.*

It was just some jealous boyfriend action. Tom Slayton—lacrosse team captain, yearbook editor—him I could picture Nora with. They'd probably live happily ever after at Los Palamos.

Except that she came here.

Tom grabbed Nora's wrist hard and pulled her toward the door. Micah tried to get in the way, but Nora stopped him. She said she didn't need rescuing, she could handle her boyfriend. Maia followed Tom and Nora out to a waiting car.

I signaled to Spike to keep playing and tried to maneuver Micah toward the stage.

"I feel like I know her," Micah said to me. We hadn't gotten to the part about Nora when we explained things earlier.

"Me, too," a voice said behind us. It was Nora. Alone. "I just want to know the truth."

There was no chance to enlighten her, though, because the lights started flashing. Lina held up her walkie and waved it frantically toward the open door of the warehouse.

Several black vans screeched to halt outside the door as I fumbled for my mobile.

Aiden didn't answer. It went straight to voice mail.

A girl can't wait for Prince Charming to rescue her ass or save the universe. *Book of Velvet*. Last Verse. Last Chapter.

LATE TO THE PARTY

AIDEN

"A concert, young lady?" Aunt Spring was livid. "Now?"

"Spring, please—" Dad warned her off. He turned to me. "The one being MemeCast?"

"Yes, our little *package* is being delivered over the Cast tonight. This dinner was just a beta test. Wait, how did you—" I dug my mobile out of my pocket. I had a very bad feeling about this.

"Green Zone knows." Dad nodded his head toward the front door. "TFC wants to stop the MemeCast because it interferes with the TFC application."

And whatever they want to stream into our heads.

"Did you tell them?" I hated to ask Dad this, but TFC could have gotten it out of him.

He shook his head. "I didn't even know about it until I overheard the Green Zone guys talking."

"It was Roger." *Forgive me*, he'd said. Roger had given up the MemeCast to save his hide.

"He was probably trying to protect his family. His parents aren't in Saigon—just like they," Dad said, nodding toward his brother, "weren't in Japan."

Uncle Brian and Aunt Spring exchanged a baffled glance.

"You were in Detention," Winter told them.

"Roger also has his little brother to look out for," Dad continued.

"Dune," I said. And Dune knew exactly where the concert was going to be.

"Velvet!" Winter cried. She grabbed my mobile and punched in the numbers. The call went straight to Velvet's voice mail.

TOO LATE FOR EVEN A NINJA WARRIOR

AIDEN

"We have to go get her," Winter pleaded.

I agreed. We were in the foyer when both Dad and Mr. Yamada stopped us.

"We're going," Winter and I said in unison.

"Green Zone," Dad whispered, motioning toward the front door.

I'd forgotten about Dad's watchdog.

"Out the back way," Mr. Yamada said. "I'll go with you."

Dad gave him the eyebrow, but Koji Yamada stifled any nonverbal objections with the wave of a hand. "You'll need a scout in case security is there."

This time Dad nodded. "Take Jao with you. I'll keep an eye on this guy."

Mr. Yamada ducked into the kitchen and reemerged

seconds later with a pair of old-style walkie-talkies, one of which he tossed to Jao. Then Winter's grandfather pulled on his no-fingered climbing gloves as he headed toward the door. "Are you coming?" he called to us.

He led us through his obstacle course and under the bleachers in the back. He pressed a panel in the chain-link fence and it slid aside effortlessly. Mr. Yamada had his own secure escape route.

Jao had parked on a street nearby so we wouldn't get blocked in. Miraculously the Bradley was still there. Winter and I piled into the back of the SUV. Mr. Yamada climbed into the front and whispered something to Jao. He nodded curtly just as if Dad had given him orders.

Even though I told him to step on it, Jao slowed the Bradley as we came up on the corner of Eighth and Salem. Winter said the Twinkie Factory was five or six blocks down. Mr. Yamada jumped out, peeked around the corner, and then motioned Jao down the block.

"This is going to take forever." I groaned.

Winter shushed me. The next thing I knew Mr. Yamada had springboarded off the hood of the black SUV onto the fire escape of a boarded-up brick building next to us. He pulled himself up the fire escape and onto the roof in one long fluid motion. Most twelve-year-old Olympic gymnasts couldn't have done it.

My jaw was scraping the pavement.

"That's my Sasuke-san." Winter beamed.

I'd never understood her pet name for her grandfather. Until now. I'd seen it once online; *Sasuke* was an old Japanese game show in which guys raced around an obstacle course. The show was named after a ninja-Samurai dude from comic books or folklore or something.

"All clear through Ninth Street," the walkie in her hand crackled.

We did this for a few more blocks. Mr. Y tarzanned over to the next building and gave us a shout out; then we crept around the block. It didn't really take long. The old man was fast. However, I couldn't bear it anymore. At the next block, I bolted out of the car, Winter on my heels. Jao honked in exasperation—or to warn Mr. Yamada. Winter and I ran the remaining blocks, hugging the shadows, until we got to the old Twinkie Factory.

• • •

It didn't matter.

We were too late. Everyone was gone. I tried Velvet again. I got the same weird not-available message that I'd gotten when I called Micah weeks ago. This was A Very Bad Thing. Catastrophic even.

Mr. Yamada caught up to us, but he didn't say a word. He just laid a hand on Winter's shoulder and pointed us into the warehouse. Jao followed.

Inside, the lights were flashing, the instruments were still on stage, and the floor was littered with plastic cups, purses. Tables were overturned.

"I wonder if anybody got out before Green Zone showed up?" Winter broke the eerie silence.

Then a noise came from under the stage. Jao went to investigate and pulled a curly-headed kid out from under the boards. A girl crawled out after him. She looked remarkably like the Nora girl from that newscast.

"Micah!" Winter ran to him. They tackle-hugged each other, exchanged a few words, and then he walked over to me. Winter and Nora, I couldn't help noticing, stared awkwardly at each other for a few seconds before following him.

"Velvet said to give you this." Micah handed me a black disk. "It ran for at least an hour, whatever that means."

He explained that when the cops came, Velvet shoved the disk into his hands and pushed him and Nora under the stage. "TFC can't know what we've done yet," she'd said. When he protested, she told him that he and Nora didn't need another stint in Detention.

Micah held out his hand and Nora took it. "Velvet said it was her turn this time," Micah whispered.

The universe quivered.

I tried calling Velvet again. Same damn message.

I sank to the curb outside the warehouse and buried my face in my hands.

I never should have involved her in this.

"She chose to help," Winter whispered as she settled on the curb next to me.

"Dude, Velvet doesn't do anything that Velvet doesn't want to do," Micah said from behind us.

"*Book of Velvet*," he and Winter said in unison.

It didn't make me feel any better.

46.0
THE REVOLUTION WILL BE CO-OPTED

WINTER

Mom chopped chicken for the *yakitori* while Dad and Grandfather watched the news. It had taken a whole lot of explaining (as well as tears, anger, and apologies) to bring everyone to this happy domestic scene. But here we were, even if we were all holding our breaths.

I handed Mom more bamboo skewers.

"Win-chan!" Grandfather yelled from the living room.

The skewers hit the floor. *This is it*, I thought. Velvet and Meme Girl had cracked before being brain-bleached. And now Green Zone was coming for us, despite all of Uncle Ichiro's added security.

The hummingbirds flittered.

Grandfather leaned into the kitchen, his mobile pressed to his ear. "Turn on the news now," he said to the person on the other end. To me, he said, "You've got to see this."

Mom and I followed him back into the living room.

Meme Girl was on the news. She sat behind the desk in her shiny suit, with her polished hair and a plastered-on smile, just like the old days.

News guy introduced her. "Coming up next: Action News welcomes back our own Rebecca Starr with a new show, The MemeCast."

No way.

Rebecca smiled and jumped right into her 'cast.

"Good evening, citizens. I know you're surprised to see me back. As some of you may know I was doing an 'independent' 'cast. Evidently my ratings were exceptional among the youth demographic.

"Meme Girl, you may be thinking, why would they want you back considering what you've been saying? Well, citizens, a wise man once said: sometimes the corporations will sell you the rope to hang them with—if it makes them enough money.

"So let's you and I be that rope."

Her smile said *trust me*, but her eyes said *don't*.

"I Will Buy You a New Life" by the Multinationals played as she cut to a commercial.

47.0
VOTE MIGNON

AIDEN

The doorbell rang, and I pulled myself out of my depressed coach-potato stupor long enough to answer it. *Security be damned.* A blonde girl in a plaid skirt, sneakers, and a Vote Mignon for Congress T-shirt stood there smiling at me.

I stared at her slack-jawed.

"Hi, I'm Anne Marie and I'd like to talk to you about voting for a great candidate."

It was her. "Velvet?"

She looked startled. "Do I know you?"

"It's me, Aiden," I said lamely. I knew there wasn't any point. I'd been erased from her mind, and they'd probably planted some memory about being a politically active prep.

Then I noticed the TFC endorsement on her T-shirt. Mignon was the guy who wanted to make the rest of the country as "safe" as Hamilton. This was the guy behind the mandatory ID program—and the chip. And here was Velvet supporting him.

And she didn't remember me. At all.

48.0
NO ELEGANT SOLUTION

AIDEN

In my dreams, I saw Velvet being dragged away by the black vans. I heard her cry for help. I saw Velvet's blank stare at my door. I saw Meme Girl bought and sold on the big screen.

And it was all my fault.

So here I stood staring at my reflection in this glossy door at TFC #23 in downtown Hamilton in the US of A.

I hardly recognized myself, but that wasn't so terrible.

My hand was on the door handle, ready.

I could forget the whole thing.

The universe was silent.

No, I can't do that to Velvet. Or Winter. Or Dad. Or me.

I stuffed my hand back into my pocket and headed toward work.

Besides, Winter and I had a plan.

It involved a certain transmitter (in a certain Scooby Doo lunch box), an underground network, a few strategically placed reflectors, and a radio tower or two.

It was a kludge, but sometimes there's no elegant solution.

12:43 AM. SOMEWHERE IN THE CITY OF HAMILTON . . .

Meme Boy, here. You're listening to the real MemeCast, citizens. Version 2.0. A few friends may be helping out with 'casts from time to time. Just think of us as little voices (inside your head or out) trying to tell you something you may not want to hear.

But don't trust us, either. There's a plague of memes out there, all trying to get inside your head.

The only voice you should really listen to is your own.

Enough of the cryptic stuff. For now.

This next song is for a girl I used to know. She's forgotten me, and more important, she's forgotten herself. But she hasn't been forgotten. This is from a new band that calls itself the Minor Bird. Here's "Anything Girl."